The M

Trouble on Teal Island

J. E. Crawford

This book is dedicated to the people who live and work on the Isles of Scilly.

First Published 2022
Mount Flagon House Publishing

Printed and bound in Great Britain
by Clays Ltd, Elcograf S.p.A.

ISBN 978-1-7397483-0-2

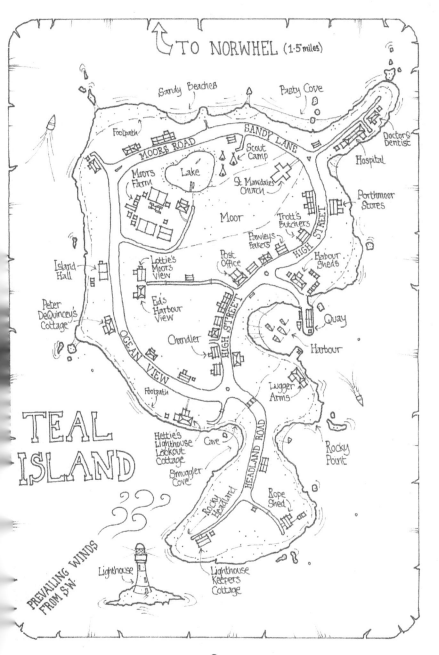

TO NORWHEL (1.5 miles)

Sandy Beaches

Pasty Cove

Footpath

MOORS ROAD

SANDY LANE

Scout Camp

Doctor & Dentist

Hospital

Moors Farm

Lake

St Mawdale's Church

Porthmoor Stores

Moor

Trott's Butchers

HIGH STREET

Pawley's Bakers

Island Hall

Lottie's Moors View

Post Office

Harbour Sheds

Peter DeQuincey's Cottage

Ed's Harbour View

Chandler

Quay

HIGH STREET

Harbour

OCEAN VIEW

Footpath

Lugger Arms

Rocky Point

TEAL ISLAND

Hettie's Lighthouse Lookout Cottage

Cave

HEADLAND ROAD

Smuggler Cove

Rocky Headland

Rope Shed

PREVAILING WINDS FROM S.W.

Lighthouse

Lighthouse Keepers Cottage

3

LIST OF CHARACTERS

Lottie (Scarlett) Pawley

Ed (Edward) Trevethick

Archie (Archibald) Bosworth

****

Hettie (Henrietta) Ennor - Archie's Great Aunt

William Duffie - Teal Lighthouse Keeper

Samuel Trevethick (Ed's Father) - Crab Fisherman

Dot Trevethick (Ed's Mother) - Crab Picker

Beryl Pawley (Lottie's Mother) - Baker

Jago Pawley (Lottie's Father) - Baker

George Trott - Butcher and Coxwain of the Lifeboat

Reverend Julian Wyatt - Vicar of St Mawdate's Church

Judith Wyatt

Wife of the Reverend Julian Wyatt

****

Henry (Hettie's Cat) - Battle-Scarred Black Tom Cat

Captain Cook - Hettie's Amazonian Parrot

Nelson - Ed's Black & White Dog

****

Douglas Bosworth - Archie's Father

Evelyn Bosworth - Archie's Mother

CHAPTER ONE
Journey to Teal Island, July 1958

Archibald Fernando Bosworth leant over the side of the island launch and experienced his three-course lunch from the train's summer menu for the second time, as it projected out over a grey, heaving sea.

Archibald's mother was sending him to stay with his Great Aunt Hettie on Teal Island for the summer holidays. 'A taste of the Atlantic would be good for you,' she had declared as she waved him off on the 10.15 a.m. '*The Cornishman*' train from Paddington to Penzance. 'Find your smile again,' she said gayly, belying her own sadness. She too could have done with a little sea air, thought Archie. His father was not at Paddington station: he was busy at the Royal Geographical Society, as he certainly didn't believe in emotional farewells. After all, Archibald was 12 now, no time for that nonsense, it was time to concentrate on his education.

Archie had endured eight and a half hours on the train, during which his mother had insisted he have the Pullman dining car lunch at 2/6 pence. 'A full tummy is a wise decision before a sea trip,' she had advised. So, 352 miles, grapefruit juice, turbot mornay, fruit melba...it all came back to him now, over the side of the boat! However, it would not be wasted: there was a vigilant seagull

5

riding on the wind beside the boat! The boat went up and down, up and down, the spray from the waves an extra bonus he didn't need. Leaning over the dark blue paint-work of this 2nd Class lugger, *Demelza*, Archie was dressed in his public school uniform of grey short flannel trousers, white cotton shirt, grey wool blazer and belted beige mackintosh, the ensemble completed by black lace-up shoes and grey woollen knee-high socks; they were all soaked! Archibald leant his head on the boat side- rail, just in time to see his grey school cap follow the lunch menu into the rolling sea.

At age 12, Archie was tall for his age: an angular face softened by a mop of brown curly hair and soft weepy hazel eyes; with his gangly arms and gangly legs, he looked in his present state like a sodden garden weed! He hoped that the wind would pick him up and carry him away – anywhere but here! A tear trickled down his cheek, which he pretended was a stray wave as it dripped onto the rail.

He had endured the train journey, followed by the British Airways *Rapide* flight to the main island airport of Nor-whel: an interminable journey, flying high over white-crested waves, during which Archie searched out tankers and sailing ships below to focus on, in order to fight his rising nausea. The plane pitched and rolled until a final bump and screech of tyres as it landed onto the runway of a rain-swept Norwhel Island, the plane's human cargo of six ashen-faced passengers, holding on for dear life. The island transfer bus ferried a shaken Archie to the quayside for another new life experience: the lugger to Teal Island, his final destination for the summer.

Archie gripped the boat rail, and at last the sea flattened and a quay came into view. So this was Teal island! The skipper tied up the launch against the grey quay steps

and helped Archie over the rail onto the granite steps.
'There, young fellow,' the skipper grinned. 'Said we'd
be there dreckly, didn't I? A bit bumpy, wasn't it, lad!' he
added with some relish.

There, at the end of the quay stood a short plump old
woman, silver grey, wiry, curly hair, flying wildly in the
wind. Archie, trying at last to raise his head, first noticed
her boots, her gathered long skirt, a huge plaid shawl
drawn around her shoulders, and finally he looked at her
face. She positively beamed, all wrinkles, a wide mouth
and bright sparkly eyes. Without hesitation, she reached
forward with both arms and embraced Archie so tightly
that he couldn't breathe, gave him a thump on the back
and said, 'Archibald, I'm your Great Aunt Hettie. Welcome to Teal island! Good heavens, lad,' she declared,
'you're grey- faced, grey-clothed and shivering. Come
on, Archibald, let's get you warmed up by Agatha!'

Archie was horrified: a train, a plane, a boat and now
some strange woman called Agatha would 'rough him
over' to finish him off! He fingered the length of scarlet
ribbon in his mackintosh pocket and felt that his heart
would break. He stooped, carrying his small brown suit-
case and the terrible secret that weighed him down from
dawn to dusk.

CHAPTER TWO

Lighthouse Lookout Cottage

Archie's wet shoes and socks were now coated, ce-
ment-like, with clogging yellow sand as he dragged
his tired feet along the track. He had hardly noticed
the flight of grey granite steps from the boat to the
quay. They had crossed cobblestones in the High
Street that were wet with mizzle, then past a number
of grey granite buildings, one with a swinging sign
blowing in the wind. After a number of these grey,
grey buildings they had turned out of the wind and
away from the cobbles, down a sandy scrub-lined
track. Archie licked his lips, which tasted of salt,
and he grimaced. After what seemed an eternity,
Hettie indicated the way by pointing to a gorse-
lined track which eventually led to a small, slate-
roofed, ancient granite cottage, entered through an
ornately carved wooden gate, more like a sideboard
front than a gate. Hettie opened the gate, stepped
over a wide granite doorstep, then ducked under a
low wooden beam that formed the roof of a small
thatched porch sheltering a monumental front door:
an ancient door with a huge brass door knocker,

shaped like a clenched fist. This was Lighthouse Lookout Cottage.

Archie stepped down into the cottage, into a small dark room with little windows and two big flowery up-holstered armchairs, where all seemed dark and smelt of wood smoke and lavender polish. Hettie went on into an adjoining room with a central wooden table, a wooden rocking chair and several unmatched carved wooden dining chairs beside a colourful cotton woven rug on the flagstone floor. Archie looked up to see a wooden clothes airer fixed to the ceiling, hanging precariously above the table and festooned with very personal items of Great Aunt Hettie's undergarments! Hettie hoisted the airer further up towards the beamed ceiling, and then moved across to a lustrous cream and chrome piece of ovenware, the like of which Archibald had never seen before.

Hettie told Archie he should take off his soaking clothes before he caught pneumonia, while she went upstairs to put a hot water bottle in his bed. Archie peeled off his mackintosh, his blazer, his jumper, his shirt and tie, his trousers, socks and shoes, wrapping himself in a huge woollen blanket. Hettie returned and told Archie to get into a large tin bath filled with steamy hot water, while she got the tea ready. Archie crouched in the chair like a drowned rat, the woollen blanket still wrapped about him. As Hettie busied herself preparing tea in the pantry area beyond the kitchen, he skilfully and swiftly took off his damp pants, dropping them on the floor. He quickly climbed into the tin bath, coiled himself up like a kitten, then put his head under the water and rather like a seal emerged with a splash, thoroughly enjoying the hot water. Hettie shouted to Archie from the pantry to put on the clean pyjamas that were warming on the cream range; they were toasty dry and soft as Archie pulled

them on. Hettie returned to the kitchen, took off her
shawl, draped it over the rocking chair and swiftly
scooped up Archie's wet clothes and dumped them all in
a large wicker basket.

'Meet Agatha!' said Hettie with a chuckle. 'Agatha, meet
Archibald!' At once the penny dropped: Agatha was this
strange oven! Oh, how warm it was here; he stroked the
front chrome rail as if it were an old friend, while Hettie
warned Archie not to touch the lids. 'Archibald, they'll
burn you, and we'll need the aloe.' Archie settled himself
in a wooden chair as Hettie lifted one of the domed
chrome lids to put a copper kettle on to boil, whilst loc-
ating a tin of Ovaltine in the pantry.

Just as Archie was raising the mug to his lips, he heard a
voice yell, 'Landlubber! Landlubber!' Startled, he looked
round for the speaker, but could see no one. Hettie
chuckled again, sipping her Ovaltine. Archie strained his
eyes and ears, then heard the voice again: 'Sacre bleu!
Sacre bleu!' Hettie jumped up from her rocking chair
and shouted towards a lean-to in the back of the cottage,
'Be quiet, Captain Cook, or I'll put you into Agatha for
our supper!' All was quiet. Archie got up and cautiously
crept into the back room. There on a wooden perch sat
an enormous multi-coloured Amazonian parrot. Archie
nearly jumped out of his skin. Captain Cook ruffled his
tail feathers and strutted up and down his perch. Hettie
came out to check that Captain Cook was not pecking at
her curtains. Archie looked aghast and muttered, 'How?
When? Why?'

Hettie tutted at the nuisance bird. 'Your Great Uncle Albert brought him back on his ship 40 years ago, and he
mimics, sometimes terrible words. He hates Henry!' Hettie chuckled once more. Archibald turned round swiftly
in his bare feet, slipping slightly. 'Henry? Who is

Henry?' This cottage was full of unidentifiable mis-matched items on shelves, walls, windowsills; surely it couldn't accommodate himself...and also a Henry?

'Oh, Henry will find you, Archibald. He'll either love you or loathe you. He hates Captain Cook – but Captain Cook was here first!' Hettie beamed conspiratorially. Archie felt battered and perplexed; in a concerned voice he said, 'But what if I don't like Henry?' Hettie raised a grey burly eyebrow and said matter of factly, 'But Archibald, he was here first!'

Before supper, now it was dusk, Hettie found some spare slippers and one of Great Uncle Albert's cardigans to keep the boy warm. She then directed Archie to where the 'necessary' was. The 'necessary' was in a small wood and granite outbuilding at the bottom of the veget-able patch. A stream fed the 'necessary' toilet cistern and the 'necessary' results went into a soak-away under the ground that Great Uncle Albert had dug some years ago. Strips of newspaper were pushed onto a nail on the wall as toilet paper. The top sheet was a newspaper page of a scandalous nature from the *News of the World*; the second sheet advertised the new musical, *My Fair Lady*. The wooden toilet seat proved to be very warm to the bottom. Returning to the cosy kitchen, they shared a supper of huge slices of crusty bread spread with butter and honey. Archibald Fernando Bosworth felt his tired eyes drooping. Hettie appeared from upstairs and handed Archie a hairbrush, announcing, 'Don't bother with your teeth tonight, Archibald, let's get you tucked into bed.'

Archie's bedroom was on the first floor, reached by a winding, narrow, creaking staircase. His room under the eaves of the cottage had huge timber beams across the ceiling, and walls covered with framed paintings of an-cient ships. Crammed on every available surface were models of ships, ships in bottles, carved masks, feathers, antlers and a plethora of items that Archie was not familiar with. Night was drawing in and his Great Aunt had switched on a lamp on his bedside cupboard. The bed had a wooden headboard of unidentifiable origin, set against the wall and facing the window opposite, The bed itself was piled high with comfy white pillows, sparkly white sheets, a tartan blanket, and topping that a huge feather eiderdown. The eiderdown cover billowed from all its feather filling, and was decorated with blue wavy patterns, both the undulating filling and the pattern echoing the sea beyond the window.

Once Archie had settled beneath this veritable mountain of comfort, warming his toes against the hot water bottle, his Great Aunt came back into the bedroom and tucked him in so tightly he could hardly breathe. Her face tanned, wrinkled and full of mischief, she whispered to Archie, 'Sleep tight, Archibald, don't let the bedbugs bite.' With that, she leant over him, kissed his sleepy forehead and left, going down the creaking wooden stairs to the cosy kitchen below.

As night fell and the sky turned dark, Archie could see the light of the Teal lighthouse from his window, flashing every 60 seconds. He counted the time between the revolving silver beams, waiting for the next to come round, rather like counting sheep, and as regular as the tick of a grandfather clock. Mesmerised by the sequence, Archibald Bosworth drifted off into the best night's sleep he had experienced for a very long time, the scarlet ribbon safely stowed in his mackintosh pocket sleeping too.

CHAPTER THREE
Archibald Meets Henry

Archie was snuggled down in bed when his Great Aunt bustled in. The sun was streaming through the cottage window, casting dancing shadows on the blue eiderdown, the blue pattern moving like waves. She was on a mission this morning: although the sun shone outside, she was dressed in a long skirt, boots and a thick *Guernsey* sweater, topped with her plaid shawl around her shoulders.

'Morning, Archibald lad, I'm on the boat to Norwhel, the island you came from yesterday, remember?' Hettie chuckled to herself. Archie winced, yes he remembered only too well, he would never eat turbot again! 'Now, porridge is in the lower oven, so is the toast. The kettle's steaming, so up you get and go exploring! If you find the heather path behind the cottage, follow that path until you reach Smuggler Cove. If you go too far, you'll know because you'll see the lighthouse keeper's cottage. That's William Duffie's, you can't miss it; Bill painted it blue last year. So, Archibald, don't get lost. Following on from the heather path, continue down the path until it narrows and drops steeply down to Smuggler Cove. Pick me some sea beet while you're there for Captain Cook.'

Archie sat up, the blanket wrapped around him. 'Will I know sea beet?' 'Definitely, if not, someone will tell you. You're never alone on a small island; even if you can't see them, they will see you!' She grinned once more, her tanned, wiry face all creased and full of wisdom. Hettie turned to leave. 'Oh, and Archibald, butter, jam and honey in the pantry, and your clothes are on HMS *Boniface*. Would you like me to bring you something back?'

Archie hesitated. 'Pencils, paper and a Sherbet Fountain, with liquorice! Please!' He had hesitated because all those things were forbidden in his house: no doodling, no cheap sweets. Obviously, Great Aunt had not been given a list of what Archie was allowed.
Actually, she had! When she had dried Archie's clothes last night, she had found the scarlet ribbon. Henrietta Ennor recognised a boy in pain when she saw one. Whatever Archibald's problem was, he would talk about it when he was ready. Until then, this boy needed few rules, and Teal Island was just the place to heal his pain. With a click of the gate latch, Hettie was gone, marching purposefully, shopping basket on arm, along the sandy scrub track, before she turned onto the High Street. The wind funnelled down the High Street and Hettie's boots clomped on the cobblestones. The quay was a world away from yesterday's weather: now sunny, bright and breezy, the air full of screeching seagulls, all following the fishing boats into the harbour – no white caps today. She climbed down the granite steps, and young Philip Trott helped her onto the launch. Hettie settled herself on a wooden bench on the port side of the boat, which would be out of the spray, her immense basket on her lap. Hettie forgot about Archibald, concentrated on her shopping list and meeting her pal Mavis for all the latest gossip.

Meanwhile, Archie was just considering where his clothes could be: certainly not on a ship nearby? However, as he was trying to solve that puzzle, something caught his eye. A huge black spider was suspended by a thin web above him. Archie was afraid of spiders, he was afraid of heights, he was afraid of deep water, he was afraid of most things! He sat rigid as the spider, huge and hairy, descended slowly, just above his head. It was at that precise moment that another black hairy thing with green eyes, perforated ears and sharp claws manoeuvred himself onto the end of his bed. Henry was a huge, black, battle-scarred tom cat. Archie was afraid of cats too. He froze. Henry stared at Archie, while Archie with palpitating heart stared at Henry. In the flash of a black silky paw, as the spider spiralled down to the eiderdown, Henry leapt and cuffed the spider onto the floor, where it rapidly escaped under the chest of drawers. Henry noted its location for a snack later. On top of the same chest of drawers was a ship in a glass case, labelled HMS *Boniface*. Archie's clothes – shorts, pants and shirt – were draped over the case.

Henry and Archie exchanged stares once more. Henry was 19 years old, survivor of many battles and romantic trysts; he was also an unusual cat, almost human in some respects. Having expended a little energy in the spider cuffing, Henry proceeded to pad his way cautiously up the eiderdown towards Archie. Archie's first reaction was to push the cat, who he assumed was the famous Henry, off the bed. However, this Henry had got rid of that huge black hairy spider, a feat for which Archie was most grateful. He said out loud, 'You must be Henry. Thank you, Henry! In return for that act of selfless bravery, come into the kitchen and let's see what we can share of Great Aunt's breakfast.'

Archie did not wash. He did not brush his hair. He got dressed and, having found everything for breakfast, he settled himself in his Great Aunt's rocking chair whilst Henry sat on the floor, near the Aga, waiting for appropriate treats for his spider removal services: a little butter, a little creamy porridge. The pair ate in silent communion.

As Archie left the cottage, Henry followed him as far as the clump of geraniums. Henry sat, washed his whiskers, washed his paws and curled up under the geraniums, the grease from the butter still glistening on his whiskers. Henry was at peace with the world, watching his pantry pal go round the back of the cottage. Butter was not usually on Henry's menu in Lighthouse Lookout Cottage, so he liked this lad. Not only would Archie be having a sherbert fountain, 'forbidden fruit', but Great Aunt's butter came from Moors Farm, which was 'forbidden fruit' to Henry. They were now partners in crime! Archibald Bosworth had survived train, plane, boat, spider and cat; he felt invincible! Time to explore!

Archie followed the heather path, the sand crunching
beneath his feet. The path was very narrow and buzzing
with insects, something else Archie didn't like. After a
few minutes he reached a granite cottage, the door and
window frames painted blue with the Trinity Lighthouse
shield above the door. It was a neat trim cottage with a
well-maintained garden and great swathes of pink holly-
hocks either side of the front door. He'd gone too far, so
Archie retraced his steps, turning back along the path.
Heather became gorse, very prickly against his legs.
Now he could feel the sea breeze on his face and the
sound of crashing waves somewhere below. This must
be the Atlantic Ocean, this must be Smuggler Cove!

All at once he was standing at the top of a small rocky
outcrop with a steep track of rocks and spiky grass leading down to a sandy cove below. Archie hesitated: it
looked a steep, dangerous path, and so far down. As he
was contemplating turning back, he noticed a figure on a
large granite rock near the water's edge, just being
washed by the incoming tide. He stood transfixed. It was
a girl, probably his age, red hair streaming behind her in
the onshore wind. Her arms were waving in the wind, as
if conducting some invisible marine orchestra: a cross
between a landed mermaid and a seaborne witch. She
had long arms, long legs with bare feet fixed on that
rock. What was she doing? He almost stumbled as he
became distracted watching her. The sun was unbearably
bright and the sea drove out all other sounds. The waves
crashed in, then pulled back, taking the sand back with

17

them, until once more a wave further out rolled, then tipped out onto the shore, almost musical in its rise and fall of sounds. But the most amazing thing that Archie couldn't believe was the turquoise colour of the sea, so clear and bright. He didn't enjoy water; he was in fear of something so dramatic, so over-powering, relentless. Archie was in awe, and intimidated, which made his feet slip, and a few small stones tumbled down the steep track to alert the girl to another's presence.

Scarlett Pawley swung round, shielding her eyes from the sun and yelled, 'Hello, you must be Archibald!'

Archie, completely taken off guard, slipped another few inches, embarrassed and frozen to the spot. He cupped his hands around his mouth and yelled back, 'How do you know who I am?' Archie was also afraid of girls.

Scarlett jumped down from the rock, her feet firmly planted on the wet sand, leaving footprints like Robinson Crusoe. She skipped towards the bottom of the steep path, and looking up, she replied, 'Of course I know you're Archibald. This is a small island, we knew who you were before you left Norwhel. Are you coming down or hovering up there for the day?'

Archie, as ever, felt useless. 'I'm afraid of heights. It looks a long way down, and I might slip and fall,' he shouted down as she stood at the bottom, looking up. 'I'm just no good at heights!'

'Or boats!' laughed Scarlett.

'Oh!' Archie gasped, his face as red as the girl's hair.

She continued shouting up at him, 'We told skipper that it was his poor boating skills that made you sick!' Scarlett laughed again, her face illuminated in the morning sun. Archie felt marooned. 'It was the turbot mornay that did it!' he defended himself in return.

Scarlett advanced, clambering confidently up the steep rocky cliff path. 'Come on, Archibald,' she said, looking him in the eyes. 'I'll help you down. Just grab hold of the thick bough on your left and come down sideways, slowly, until the next handgrip on your right.'

Archie returned her assertive gaze and sighing deeply, saying, 'Do I have any choice?'

'No!' Scarlett grinned.

Archie edged slowly down, finding handholds on the tree branches until he reached Scarlett's outstretched hand. As he took her hand, he noted she had a really firm grip, like a boy's! Once he was safely down, Scarlett looked at his sandalled feet.

'Shoes off and we'll see what our ocean canvas has for us today,' she said, looking directly into Archie's hazel eyes; Scarlett's were blue-green, rather like the sea.

'Canvas?' Archie echoed.

'Oh yes, every day, as the tide turns, the beach reveals new treasures for the taking,' she informed him enthusiastically. 'Come, walk with me'.

Archie followed, rather like a faithful puppy in the presence of a great mistress. 'See!' Scarlett held up a brown, plastic-looking pocket. 'Archibald, this is a Mermaid's Purse,' and promptly passed it to Archie.

He looked confused. 'But, there are no such things, are there? And please don't call me Archibald, it's Archie.'

'Well, Archie,' she continued, 'it's the egg case of a dog-fish: those little tendrils on the edges once held onto seaweed, beneath the waves.'

Archie was entranced and, following Scarlett, he bent down to seek out new discoveries. In the space of half an hour they found countless shells: cockles, limpets, pastel-coloured periwinkles and a huge scallop shell. They picked up many types of skeleton, and finger- like seaweeds, slimy from the receding tide. Scarlett showed Archie how to pop the bubbles on the bladderwrack seaweed to make a satisfying pop, which made Archie laugh. 'Why does it have those bumps?' he asked.

Scarlett peered at the seaweed in his hand and replied, 'It helps it float, Archie, in the forest on the sea floor, before it breaks away to the surface in the tides.'

An oyster catcher followed them: a delicate little coastal bird, pecking at the wet sand, wading into the shallows for a lunch of worms. Archie stood on the shore, carefully handling an orange periwinkle; and as an aside, he said to himself, 'Such thick shells for something so beautiful.'

Scarlett looked him in the eye and with some emphasis said, 'Everything on Teal needs to have a tough shell to survive, Archie.' Her face coloured a little, but she turned away so he couldn't see it. 'You never told me your name, and yet you seem to know a lot about me,' he said. She turned to face Archie. 'It's Scarlett, Archie, but I prefer Lottie. It's the hair, you see.' With that, she flicked her hair back very theatrically with a giggle.

Archie looked thoughtful. 'Lottie, do you think Great Aunt knew you would be here this morning?'

Lottie looked at him knowingly. 'Auntie Hettie knows everything, Archie. She is respected by all'.

Archie considered Lottie's answer. 'She's gone to Norwhel today to shop,' he said.

Lottie looked at Archie, her mouth turned up at the corners. 'Oh yes, the shopping, but also a pint at the Lugger's Arms with her pal Mavis Penworth, both postwoman and the best source of gossip on the islands!' They both laughed. 'Come on, Archie, she asked you to pick some sea beet for that foul-mouthed parrot of hers, yes?'

Archie no longer felt surprised at Lottie's psychic knowledge of his life, so grinned and replied, 'And as if I knew what that is!' Lottie led Archie to a sheltered corner of the cove and retrieved a small basket. 'Early lunch, Archie?' she asked, proffering the unwrapped contents of crusty bread and egg mayonnaise sandwiches.

Archie was surprised how hungry he was and sat down on the rock beside her. 'Lottie, the bread here on Teal is amazing; is it from a local bakery?'

'Oh yes,' Lottie replied without enthusiasm, 'third-generation bakers!'

As Archie bit into the sandwich, carefully extracting some grass, he asked, 'Lottie, what were you doing when I arrived, on the rock?'

Lottie looked away into the distance and replied, 'I was wishing to the wind, Archie, screaming my hopes and

21

dreams to the seven seas, hoping they would return fulfilled.'

Archie looked puzzled. 'Do you really believe that could work?' he said.

She returned her gaze to his. 'Archie, I'd try anything. It seems that no one else is listening, so I might as well send my dreams out to sea; it beats a message in a bottle.' She got up, wiped her mouth, folded up the napkin in the basket and rapidly changed the subject. 'OK, beet time, Archie, and let's get you back up the cliff path!'

So Archie wasn't the only one with secrets.

CHAPTER FIVE
Lottie and Archie meet William Duffie, the Lighthouse Keeper

Lottie climbed up the cove cliff face first, then went back to pull Archie up to the top. She had a really strong grip. Archie wasn't skilled at any sport, climbing or otherwise, and was bullied by his peers as 'Awkward Archibald' or worse. He had compromised by being a line judge at rugby and an umpire at tennis. He was very observant at 'watching' rather than 'doing'. And Archie was not competitive; he didn't care whether he won or lost, as long as he could join in. This made him unpopular with teachers and boys alike.

Lottie had to help her mum Beryl that afternoon, but as they were walking back, Lottie suggested they divert a little to visit the lighthouse keeper as his cottage wasn't far away. William Duffie was busy painting his gate when Lottie and Archie approached. Teal island locals loved to talk and be just plain nosey. Therefore after Lottie had said a customary 'Hello, Mr Duffie,' William carefully laid his paintbrush across the top of his paint pot and with a wide, knowing smile countered with, 'And good day to you, Scarlett!'

William was a semi-retired lighthouse keeper, having spent most of his working life either at sea or as keeper of the lights off the Scottish islands. Stocky, broad-shouldered, with a face tanned by years of a life out-doors, weathered and wise, Mr Duffie had alert, brown eyes, belying his seventy-five years, his head crowned by an impressive covering of thick, curly silver-grey hair with matching beard and moustache: he was the very image of a seafaring man. William Duffie was also a walking encyclopaedia of all marine and seafaring knowledge, and he had a way of standing, feet apart, shoulders square, that suggested that even a strong wind couldn't budge him.

Archie felt conflicted, he was in awe of this solid grey badger of a man, who radiated wisdom, and yet when he spoke you didn't feel he was treating you like a child, talking down to you as other grown-ups did. It felt like a kind of level playing field: Archie didn't perceive Mr Duffie as old, and Archie didn't feel like a child. Looking directly at Archie, William said, 'Well, young man, you must be Archibald, Aunt Hettie's great neph-ew!'

Archie leant back, and before William could say another word, Archie blushed, lowered his eyes and replied, 'Yes, sir, the one who wasted his lunch over the side of the *Demelza* yesterday.'

William looked Archie over carefully, and after hesitat-ing, said, 'Och, lad, don't worry about that. Firstly, it wasn't wasted on the birds and fish; and secondly,' William looked directly at Archie, 'lad, you were out of sorts for 20 minutes; but your Great Uncle Albert was sick for 20 days, his first time at sea!'

Archie looked surprised. '20 days! Why didn't he stop going to sea if it made him so ill, Mr Duffie?'

William picked up his paintbrush once more, carefully taking a piece of bracken out of the brush and returning Archie's gaze. He said, 'Well, Archibald, he wanted to be a sailor and sail the seven seas far more than he wanted to be sick!'

Archie's face lifted, in fact one eyebrow did too. After a few seconds, Archie summoned up his courage and said, 'Mr Duffie, can I ask you a question?' William beamed. 'Och, lad, I love questions!'

Archie held the beet in one hand and gestured towards the lighthouse with the other. 'Mr Duffie, I see your lighthouse at night through my bedroom window, and I wondered how many steps there were to the light?'

William put the brush down again, once more across the pot lid. 'Well, Archibald, there are 100, but some of those form two platforms: the first to the bunk room, the second lands at the kitchen. The final flight of stairs lead to the light itself, in the tower. The lower area on the ground level is for storage, the motors and where the stairs begin; these are now metal, but they were wood many years ago.'

Archie was fascinated. 'So, Mr Duffie, do you sleep there at night?'

'Yes, I do, Archibald, except for my day off, today, when a relief keeper comes over from Norwhel.'

Archie was unstoppable. 'Does the lighthouse shake when the storms come, Mr Duffie?'

William stroked his beard thoughtfully. 'Well, lad, the kitchen and living area are nearest the top, and yes, the tower does shake at times.' He was obviously enjoying giving Archie the whole scary keeper's experience today! Then, changing the subject to include Scarlett, William directed his conversation to her: 'What treasures did you find on the beach today, Scarlett?'

Lottie was very fond of Mr Duffie, as he treated her like an intelligent 12-year-old. 'A nice intact mermaid's purse, Mr Duffie,' she replied.
'No driftwood then?' he continued. 'No, Mr Duffie, Smuggler's Cove was swept clean.'

Always keen to impart local knowledge, William looked at them both. 'Ah well, we'll need a good storm before we get nice pieces of wood.'

Archie looked at Lottie, bewilderedly. 'What do you do with the wood, Lottie? Is it for the fire?'

Lottie joined William, looking a little conspiratorial, 'Oh,' she replied, 'anything it wants to be!'

William laughed, but looking at Archie's face, he said, 'Wait a moment.' He disappeared into his cottage and after a minute returned with a piece of weathered wood, about a foot long, washed smooth by the sea, exposing knots and wood grain. William handed it to Archie. 'Young man, fashion it how you like.'

Archie held the wood in his free hand and with bright eyes asked, 'What do you think it will make, Mr Duffie?'

William patted Archie's shoulder. 'Whatever you want it to be, Archibald.' He continued, 'Would you care to come and take some tea and cakes with me next week and I could tell you more of a lighthouse keeper's life? I make a good rock cake, I'm told!'

Archie was, for once, keen and inquisitive, and as William picked up his paintbrush again, he beamed and replied, 'Yes please, Mr Duffie!'
'OK, lad,' William beamed back. '11 a.m. next Friday, and don't be late. I've got some serious fishing to fit in later that afternoon from my boat, the *Lively Lady*, plenty of mullet about now!' With that, William returned to his painting and Lottie and Archie walked back to Lighthouse Lookout Cottage.

As they reached the back gate, Lottie opened it and said, 'Right, Archie, tomorrow is Saturday. Be at Pawley's Bakers in the High Street by 11. Saturday, it's a tradition you should enjoy.' As she turned to go, she put her hand in her shorts pocket and gently pulled out the mermaid's purse to put in Archie's breast pocket of his shirt. 'A small beach treasure to remember your first cliff descent,' she said ceremoniously, and with that she closed the gate as Archie went in, and hurried along the path to meet her mum in town.

Archie gently felt the mermaid's purse and gazed after Lottie as she disappeared from view.

CHAPTER SIX
Crab Cakes, Shrews and a Ditty Box

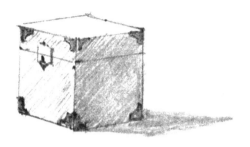

Archie went into the cottage. He was alone, but the cottage was full of memories: photos, paintings, strange pieces of furniture. Archie headed straight for Agatha, but it was empty!

Henry appeared, as if by magic: time to hunt out lunch. 'Well, Henry, it must be the pantry.' The pair went through the kitchen to explore the shelves of Great Aunt's pantry: jars and jars of unidentified ingredients; tins of sardines, a lidded butter dish, a meshed box of cheese pieces, large enamelled lidded tins of flour; and at the front of the top shelf, a big round tin with a picture of the Queen's coronation on the lid. Archie prised the lid off and the smell of jam and butter wafted out – it was a huge jam sponge! 'Well,' Archie declared, looking at Henry who was now in the pantry with him, 'that's for dessert.'

Archie searched further: on the flagstone floor he found a huge earthenware pot with a metal lid that looked interesting. He lifted the lid and peered in. 'Ah, bread, perfect!' He found a glass and poured himself a glass of ginger beer from a jug on the bottom shelf. A veritable banquet! Archie collected together the bread, butter and cheese and put them on the kitchen table. Henry followed the cheese aroma. A large dark wood dresser held flowery china plates, so he took one down. The drawer beneath the dresser shelves held the knives and forks. The bread board lay on the kitchen table with the bread knife. Everything was ready.

Archie settled into his Great Aunt's chair and placed his piece of driftwood and the mermaid's purse beside his plate for further study while he munched. He sliced the bread and cheese, cutting a small chunk for Henry with the addition of a spot of butter. As Archie was chewing a buttered slice of crusty bread, both he and Henry had their silence interrupted by Captain Cook squawking 'Picoler! Picoler!' Archie nearly choked with laughter: he enjoyed his French lessons at school, as Monsieur Devoir was really funny and taught all sorts of vocabulary to 12-year-olds! 'Picoler' translated as, booze! 'Shut up, Captain Cook!' Archie barked to the lean-to where the parrot lived. Silence.

Never had Archie been left to choose his own lunch. Oh, and that cake! Archie scraped the breadcrumbs off his plate, leaving space for a slice of that sponge. The bread knife squished through the jam; Archie wiped his finger along the rim of the jam jar, then licked off the strawberry jam. Henry settled by Agatha, and Archie turned the piece of driftwood over in his hands. What could it be and how to carve it?

Archie was a tidy lad, bludgeoned into neatness throughout his twelve years, so he washed up the lunch things and put them onto the wooden drainer to dry. With an afternoon to himself, Archie wandered about the cottage, sipping his ginger beer. He studied the huge inglenook fireplace, with what looked like a ship's mast for the beam above it. There were endless cupboards,

29

and shelves with numerous china knick-knacks, including a jug identified as 'A Gift From Penzance'. He tried out a rather tempting window seat in the lounge, where he drained his glass. He opened drawers, enjoying the sensation of being a novice curator at this marine museum of sailing memories and framed faded photographs of fishing folk from a bygone age. He compared it with his own home in London, which was quite modern and crammed with books piled everywhere, more like a library than a home.

Eventually Archie went up into his bedroom and poked about. Underneath some naval flags he uncovered a large wooden chest with the initials A.A.E. Lifting the heavy lid, he felt he had opened a letter from the past. His Great Aunt's cottage smelt of wood smoke, furniture polish and lavender, but as Archie lifted the chest lid he breathed in trapped sea air, musty rags and some sort of spice he couldn't trace. The inside of the lid was painted in a simple way, with a three-masted sailing ship set against a perfect blue sky. As Archie turned his attention to the inside of the chest, he reckoned he had never seen so many strange random objects. A smaller upper half-shelf at the top of the chest was home for smaller, more precious items: a delicate pearl-handled penknife, a brown leather-bound prayer book and a steel-cased pocket watch.

Further down the chest was a small wood-handled axe, now rather rusty; a large seed pod the size of an apple; two nutmegs, now rather aged; a conch shell; some black wooden, carved exotic animals and a tarnished silver frame of a young woman sitting very sedately, almost frozen on a huge armchair. She looked familiar to Archie. There was a clay pipe; a carved ivory button; a small coil of rope with a metal whistle attached, also rusty; some large rusty needles and thick waxy thread; 6 blue

buttons with an anchor design; a neckerchief of thick
linen and a dark blue woollen hat. Towards the bottom of
the chest lay a delicate linen drawstring bag. Archie carefully undid the strings and took out a fine cotton
handkerchief embroidered with blue flowers and the initials H.S.E. What an assortment! He resisted the temptation to blow the whistle, and carefully packed everything
away where he had found it. However, he forgot to replace the naval flags on top of the chest.

Archie picked up a book from a shelf entitled *Salty Dog
Yarns* and escaped the gloom of the cottage for the sunny
garden, where he settled himself on what appeared to
have been an old church pew. He read three pages, then
promptly fell asleep, Henry curled up beside him.

Sometime after five o'clock Hettie returned from Norwhel, laden with groceries, a newspaper, Archie's paper,
pencils, a Sherbet Fountain and fresh gossip. She woke
Archie, gave him his shopping from Porthmoor Stores
and a fresh glass of ginger beer, and began making supper. Archie watched with fascination as Hettie mixed
something white, fleshy and fishy with some mashed
potatoes. She shaped them into round flat cakes and
popped them into Agatha, topped with butter. From Hettie's voluminous basket she extracted some green weeds.
Archie looked on, horrified, as she appeared to be frying
the weeds! He sat at the kitchen table transfixed by these
odd ingredients.

Hettie looked at him bemused. 'Trevethick Crab Cakes
Archibald,' she explained, 'are a Friday tradition in the
summer. Well, fish generally is, but I wasn't sure how
you'd cope with heads, fins and tails today, especially ...'
and she paused, 'after that cake!' Archie coloured: Great
Aunt knew everything! 'Local crab, Archibald, caught,

cooked and picked today, and samphire from the beach at Norwhel. Try it!'

Archie tried a little with some vinegar and pepper. 'Oh, Great Aunt, it's like green beans but tastier. It's all right, not slimy, and the crab cakes are yummy, not fishy at all.'

Evening dinner finished, Archie visited the 'Necessary' and brushed his teeth in the kitchen china sink, drying his mouth on the nearby towel. After struggling into his Agatha-warmed pyjamas, he carefully put his mermaid's purse and the piece of driftwood on his chest of drawers. Hettie bustled in and noticed that the naval flags were out of place.

'Oh, Archibald, you found your Great Uncle's Ditty Box! Albert, Archibald, Ennor: A.A.E.'

Archie looked apologetic. 'I hope you didn't mind, Great Aunt.' Had he been too nosey? 'Oh, not at all, lad, it's a bit of your history too.'

'What is a Ditty Box?' asked Archie.

Hettie sighed and smiled. 'Well, Archibald, it's a sailor's box of keepsakes, useful items and memories of home.'

'Who was the girl in the photo?'

'That, Archibald, was me, many moons ago. In a way, I travelled with Albert over the seven seas, even though I never left these islands. The handkerchief was mine, a love token, it was all the thing then.' Hettie opened the lid, retrieved the penknife and put it on the chest of drawers next to the driftwood, the mermaid's purse, the pencils and the paper. 'I think you could use your Great

Uncle's knife to fashion something from this piece of driftwood. No Sherbert till tomorrow, Archibald Bosworh!' she said, wagging her finger and smiling.

'Thank you, Great Aunt,' gushed Archie, quite overcome with the attention he'd had raining in on him today. Hettie tucked him in tight, advised him again about the bed bugs and bustled out.

Archie lay as darkness came, watching the lighthouse light revolving. He now pictured William in his bunk or drinking cocoa in the kitchen, snug each night, keeping that light revolving, keeping the ships safe out in the dark blue night on the rolling dark blue ocean. Archie hadn't thought about the ribbon all day, the first time he could let his heart lighten for many a month.

CHAPTER SEVEN
Treasure Boxes and Cheeky Shrews

Archie woke up, the sun streaming through his bedroom window, reflecting a shaft of rainbow colours onto his chest of drawers and also – crikey! – that cat on the end of his bed. Henry opened one eye and challenged Archie to repel him. Archie sat up. He had not slept well, his head full of things that Teal Island had shut out. He thought he remembered feeling something coming into the room, in the dark last night, so it was Henry. Archie's mother didn't like cats, but he remembered they had one once; he even remembered the name, Lolly, which made him shake off a remembered sadness.

Archie went downstairs and wandered into the kitchen, the sound and smell of something sizzling coming from Agatha's simmer ring. A heavy frying pan was smoking and some spitting came from a pair of potato cakes. Archie watched appreciatively as his Great Aunt cracked two eggs with dark yellow yolks into the space beside the potato cakes. He watched the transparent gel of the eggs turn white before Hettie turned them over with a wooden spatula, and nudged an egg and a potato cake onto a warmed plate for Archie.

34

Henry appeared; he lay on the floor near a china dish, a dish with the remains of some crab from last night's supper.

Archie started stuffing, watching Henry, and with his mouth still full said, 'Great Aunt, why isn't Henry eating his breakfast?'

Hettie filled her own plate and looked at Henry. 'He's waiting for the thief.'

'What thief?'

'Archibald, we have a shrew living under the dresser behind you. It likes to help itself to Henry's suppers and lunches. Henry is waiting to catch it.'
All at once, a little pointy-nosed, light-brown, mouse-like visitor appeared from under the dresser. Henry was fast and pounced, but he missed his prey, who promptly returned to its dresser home. Henry then finished his crab, and having had a little fun, padded outside to the garden for a well-earned rest, after a thorough whisker, paw and bottom wash.

Archie had devoured every last scrap of his breakfast, helped wash the dishes, then followed Hettie into the back garden. On one side were rows of runner beans clambering up structures like Indian teepees, adorned with bright red flowers; Hettie was pulling off the beans that hid amongst the flowers, and Archie found it all a beautiful, calming sight.

He went back into the gloom of the cottage to fetch his paper and pencils, then sat down on the pew in the warm sun to sketch the bean poles, the flowers and his Great Aunt attending to them lovingly, as if she was nurturing a small child or a lamb, humming to herself a song from a wartime memory. Archie closed his eyes and just listened: there were bees buzzing, blackbirds singing, bushes rustling in the wind; Archie breathed in the salty sea air and felt joy.

Just before eleven, Archie told Hettie that he was meeting Lottie. He described how he'd met her yesterday at Smuggler Cove, how she stood on a rock shouting and how they had beachcombed for treasure.

Hettie interrupted, 'Oh, so she found the sea beet for you!' 'Yes, and we met Mr Duffie, the lighthouse keeper, and he has invited me back next Friday to tell me about a lighthouse keeper's life. Is that all right?'

Hettie fondly patted his mop of brown curly hair and replied, 'Yes, Archie, so long as I get a rock cake, if he makes them. Lighthouse keepers make great cooks: it's all that maintenance time, you see!'

Archie went back to his bedroom to fetch the mermaid's purse. He held it out to show his Great Aunt. She peered at it and looking into the distance said, 'I may have just the thing for that.' She disappeared into her bedroom and after a few minutes returned with a small, what appeared to be home-made wooden box. The box had a neatly shaped crab carved into its lid, and polished smooth. It was obviously very old and smelt of the same spice that Archie had smelt from his Great Uncle's ditty box when he'd lifted the lid.

'There, my dear,' Hettie said gently, 'that'll make a handsome box, just right for your treasures. That's your own ditty box, Archibald. You see, in olden times, sailors all had their own boxes; if they died at sea, the box was returned to the sailor's family. It usually held essentials for a sailor's life on ship: needles, strong thread for re-

pairing sails and clothes, buttons for repairing their uniform, always a penknife. Sailors had a lot of spare time,
especially if the wind dropped or if they were on watch.
There would be a good hat and neckerchief for shore
landings, a comb, a razor, although most ships had their
own barber or appointed barber. Then, Archibald, there
would be space for keepsakes from mothers and sweet-
hearts, because sailors would sometimes be away from
home for months. Such journeys over time with so many
ports: each would provide a treasure or memento of their
journey across the oceans.' Archibald put the mermaid's
purse into the box. 'Thank you, Great Aunt Hettie, I shall
make this my memory box.'

A muffled 'good' was Hettie's response, as she handed
Archie some pocket money to go to Porthmoor Stores.
With that, Hettie sniffed and wiped a moist eye with her
hankie, always tucked up her sleeve for such emergen-
cies, and returned to her beans. Hettie and Albert had
never had children of their own. The islanders called her
Auntie Hettie as a sort of honourable title. Everyone
loved her, and in many ways she'd helped rear many
children, and Archie was fast becoming one of them.

Archie carefully carried the box to his room and placed
it on the chest of drawers. He left by the cottage front
gate, turned down the heather path, then the gorse lane
and into the High Street. The path ceased to crunch under his feet as smooth cobblestones carried his feet along
to the busy shops.

CHAPTER EIGHT
A Saturday Tradition and Archie meets Edward

As Archie passed down the High Street, the breeze from the harbour made him turn up the collar of his shirt. This was his first visit to the main shopping area of Teal, and he made a mental note of what was where. The buildings were clustered together, cheek by jowl, all constructed of the same grey granite, flat-faced, only doorway and window styles showing the passage of time and building styles. The harsh grey granite was relieved by window boxes of geraniums, tubs of blue flowering plants and gaily painted signs swinging in the wind. Although the sun was shining, the cobbles beneath Archie's feet and the weathered architecture suggested harsher times.

The High Street was busy today: mothers with children, young lads on bicycles, a hand cart, a donkey munching one of the flower tubs and several barking dogs. Looking through an alleyway to the harbour side, he watched several old men with grey beards and weather-beaten faces, puffing on pipes, perched on large wooden crates, animatedly putting the world to rights.

What Archie noticed was that unlike the city, where people hurried by and always seemed to be engaged in some urgent business, here on Teal women stood chattering, laughing, shopping bags in one hand, impatient children in the other. The smell of fish and the sea circulated around the cheerful shoppers, making it more of a social occasion than shopping. It was as if time was standing still, like a slow-motion film. Archie watched a butterfly land on a young woman's shoulder, unobserved. The shoppers seemed oblivious to the chill wind: faces were ruddy, tanned, women's headscarves knotted tightly. Every man wore a Breton cap or woolly hat and boots, prepared for the weather. Further down the High

Street, Pawley Baker's could not be mistaken, or indeed missed. The wonderful smell of freshly baked bread drew you towards its door. Archie breathed it in, the bread smell making him feel hungry once more. All he seemed to have done since he arrived was eat and sleep! Sitting patiently on the cobbles outside the bakery door was a rather scruffy black and white, mixed parentage dog. Archie bent down to pat its wiry head and received a lick as reward.

A bell jangled as Achie opened the door to the bakery. Behind the long wooden counter was a face he recognised: Lottie. Stood close to Archie by the counter was a young boy, about Archie's age, he guessed. Behind Lottie, were open shelves full of an assortment of crusty loaves and rolls. Under the wooden counter in front of her were glass-fronted cabinets showing off shelves of delicious cakes: rock cakes, madeleines, jam sponge slices, treacle tarts, jam tarts both yellow and red, ginger parkin, egg custards, eccles cakes and last of all, doughnuts, freshly fried and coated in sugar.

There were other customers in the shop, and Lottie was serving behind the counter with two other, older people: a woman and a man. They were all swiftly taking orders and putting cakes into paper bags, the bread placed directly into shopping baskets. The star turn this morning was undoubtedly the doughnuts: oh, the sugary, doughy smell made Archie's mouth water. Small children tugged at mothers' hands and big sisters' skirts, repeatedly pleading, 'Buy me, buy me!'

Lottie looked at the woman beside her and said, 'Can I go now, mum? my friends are here.' Archie put two and two together and realised the woman was Lottie's mum and Lottie's family ran the bakers. Archie remembered Lottie's comment at Smuggler's Cove: 'third generation-bakers'. Lottie's mum lowered her glasses onto the end of her nose, peering over the top of them. She had her dark brown hair tied back in a bun, a large white apron covering her ample frontage; beneath the apron, a pale blue jumper. She had large hands, very red. Her countenance was not cheerful. Lottie's mum looked strained: a pinched face that resembled one of the cottage loaves, puffed, glossy and at odds with Lottie's slim face and red lustrous hair, neatly tied today in a ponytail.

The man, Archie guessed, would be Lottie's dad: a jolly man, red-faced, red hair, red sideburns, baker's white cap, white apron; he was literally covered in flour! He was like a jolly advertisement for something tasty in a pie shop. In the corner of his mouth he chewed absent-mindedly on an unlit pipe, rather like a plump Popeye.

Lottie looked imploringly at her mum, 'Please mum!'

Beryl Pawley returned a more concentrated look. 'Very well, Scarlett, but be back by four, I've meat to prepare for Monday. Oh,' she added, 'and Scarlett, one doughnut each and none for Nelson; doughnuts are bad for him!'

As her mum turned away to serve a customer, wiping her hands on her apron, Lottie put three doughnuts in a bag and swiftly added a sausage roll from the shelves underneath the counter. Lottie licked her fingers, removed her apron and hung it up, and motioned to Archie and the boy next to him, gesturing with her thumb towards the bakery door.

40

CHAPTER NINE
Pasty Cove and a Saturday Tradition

As swift as the seagulls that screeched overhead looking for snacks, the group of three plus the dog hastened right, further along the High Street, past the Lugger's Arms, Trott's, the butcher and Porthmoor Stores, to a path opposite some terraced cottages. It led down a sandy path to hilly sand dunes, thick with rye grass and broom, and on down to a sheltered sandy cove.

Here they all sat down, their backs against the dunes: Lottie in the middle, between Archie and the other boy. Lottie removed her sandals and settled the dog in the shade of a group of rocks. She cleared her throat and spoke ceremoniously, 'Archibald Bosworth, meet Edward Trevethick, oh and Nelson, our companion, trusted adviser and snack consumer.' Nelson, as if on prompt, sat up, licked his whiskery mouth to reveal a row of white needle- sharp teeth, and barked joyfully before sitting down once more, staring longingly at Lottie's bakery bag.

'Right', said Lottie in a businesslike manner. 'Saturday traditions hold, lads: you consume the delicious freshly baked Saturday doughnut, with no licking of lips, wiping of mouths or licking fingers.' Turning to Archie, she added, 'This is a serious test, Archie, a test that you must pass as an initiation ceremony into the Pasty Cove Saturday Doughnut Club.' Lottie reached into the paper bag and passed one sugar-coated doughnut to Archie, one to Edward and the last she took for herself. Nelson yelped, partly because he'd like some doughnut and partly because he was confirming his club membership. They began, each biting into the warm dough, sugar spilling down their shorts, the sugar inevitably coating their mouths and chins. 'Remember, Archie, no licking!' Lottie added, between bites. All three laughed and scoffed with every bite.

Archie squealed, 'This is terrible, I so want to lick my mouth!' All three sat back, in the dunes, laughing and shouting, waving arms, stamping legs, sugar coating their faces, their shirts, their hands; they looked as if they had all had a parcel of sugar thrown at them. After a few minutes of riotous laughter, Lottie held one arm aloft and shouted, 'OK, now you wipe!' All three frantically wiped the sugar from their faces on to the back of their hands, licked their lips, licked their fingers, wiped their hands on their shorts, whilst Nelson sat patiently, licking his lips. Lottie passed the sausage roll to Nelson, and whilst the three lay back in the sand laughing, Nelson gulped down the sausage roll and then began rolling over in the sand, snapping at the sand hoppers.

As they lay on their backs, looking upwards, the sky was a perfect blue; the sea, at low tide, far out today, was a turquoise blue. It was difficult to see where the sea ended and the sky began. It was what was known locally as a blue, blue day.

After a few minutes of quiet contentment, Lottie turned to Archie and said, 'Edward prefers to be called Ed. However, if he is mean to me, I call him Eduardo!'

Ed laughed and turned to Archie saying, 'I assume you don't want to be called Archibald, Archie?'

'No, especially not my full name.' Both Lottie and Ed looked at Archie, awaiting further information. Archie continued, 'My full name is Archibald Fernando Bosworth,' and he grinned. Ed sat up, smiling widely. 'Whatever made your parents call you that, Archie? Is it a family name, sort of aristocratic?'

Archie sat up, hugging his knees, squinting into the bright sun, a few sugar crumbs still lingering on his chin. 'I'm named after a volcano in the Galapagos Islands, where my parents had their honeymoon.'

Lottie, warming to the subject, licked her lips once more but sat up to continue the interrogation. 'Archie, why did your parents name you after a volcano? Did you have a large mouth or big nostrils like the cone on a volcano?'

Archie laughed. 'Nothing as simple as that. My parents are vulcanologists...they investigate volcanoes for a living.'

There was a long silence from Lottie and Ed. Lottie broke the silence. 'Beats my parents as bakers; perhaps I can call them bakerologists!' They all laughed, but Ed was very quiet.

Archie leaned forward and spoke to Ed. 'What do your parents do, Ed?'

Ed pursed his lips and looked downcast at the beach. 'Fourth-generation crab fishermen.' There was no opportunity to continue the joke, and the mood was sombre. Archie studied the boy sitting next to him: there was a sadness in his bent shoulders that struck Archie as familiar personal territory. Ed was tall, long-limbed, knobbly-kneed, sticking out ears on a long thin face, long nose, long chin. Freckles decorated the face and the whole lengthy ensemble was crowned with a mop of straight fair hair over eyebrows that hardly showed, and eyes that were indiscernibly blue. Ed looked up at Archie; the eyes were not tranquil but sharp, clear, searing, intelligent. Archie felt Ed could see straight through him, to his soul and knew his secret.

Lottie broke the awkward silence, 'Anyway, Archie, at least Ed hasn't told us the history and recipe of doughnuts, the story of the granite rocks beside us, the weather in the clouds, etcetera etcetera!'

Archie looked bewildered. 'Why would he do that, Lottie?' he questioned.

'Because, Archie, two years ago, Eduardo here broke his leg and dislocated his hip, falling off a rock at Lugger Point!'

'But what does that have to do with all that stuff you said?' continued Archie.

'Well, confined to his bed and his cottage, my cousin here was given his grandfather's encyclopaedias to look at.'

'And so?' quizzed Archie.

Ed continued Lottie's narrative of his bed-bound winter in his cottage. 'At first, Archie, I used the books to kill the spiders. Then I stacked them up and ran my dinky cars under their splayed spines. Eventually I started reading them, and it was like I'd been starved of knowledge for all my life. I read and drank it all in; I became obsessed with them.'

'And so,' interjected Lottie, 'our lives, Archie, will be embroidered, no splattered, with his encyclopaedic knowledge, you'll see!' After a few minutes watching Nelson digging in the sand, Ed looked towards the horizon and, knitting his brows together, said, 'Examining the sand here reminds me that, in case you were interested, the Romans produced glass from the 1st century. They made it from sand, well-crushed quartz and added some evaporated soda from lakes that had dried up; fascinating!' Ed stopped talking and, as if by magic, returned his attention to the sands of Pasty Cove.

There was a long pause, during which Lottie covered both her eyes with her hands and shook her head. 'Archie, don't encourage him or we'll hear the history of doughnuts, and I'd rather eat them than learn about their history; I spend enough time making them!' They all laughed.

Archie turned to Lottie: 'You make the doughnuts, Lottie?' He sounded more impressed than interested in their manufacture.

'Well, Archie, I make the dough, I knead them, fry them, sugar them, sell them. I know all about baking, Archie; third-generation baker, that's me!'

Again, the quiet space afterwards, followed by a knowing look between the two cousins and Archie saw it: the two cousins had jobs to do in the afternoon, so they all got up, brushing the sand from their legs and feet.

Before they left the beach, Archie turned to Ed, directing his attention to Nelson: 'Ed, why is he called Nelson? Is it a family thing, or was it from your books?'

Ed raised one fair eyebrow, looked at Lottie, looked down at the scruffy doe-eyed doggie misfit and replied, 'He's named after Vice-Admiral Horatio Nelson, the famous British naval commander who was hit in his arm with a musket ball during an assault on Tenerife, so he was armless. Look at Nelson, Archie; he's hardly dangerous, and he's 'armless too!' Ed leant against Lottie and the pair were suffused with giggles.
After a moment, Archie got the joke and laughed with them. Nelson felt sure all this attention meant there was more food...but he got lots of strokes instead.

CHAPTER TEN
Porthmoor Stores and Archie meets Peter De Quincey

The three left Pasty Cove and parted company at the
High Street. Archie thanked Lottie for the doughnuts and
Ed for his lesson on Roman glass.

Porthmoor Stores was a substantial, two-storey building
made of large granite blocks; Archie wondered if giant
islanders had carried those here. There was no porch, but
an archway beside the stores from where Archie could
smell what he was sure were 'horses doings'. There were
small windows, of which even the mullions were made
of granite. The windowsills were slate, now weathered
with grey lichen. The front door, which was fastened
open, was the biggest, thickest piece of wood Archie had
ever seen: a perfect partner for the giant granite blocks of
the building itself. Archie stepped over the granite hearth
and into the past, into a shop smelling strongly of soap
powder and paraffin.

The floor was made of smoothed giant flagstones, worn
smooth by years of passing feet; and the walls were lined
floor to ceiling with wooden shelves, stacked and tum-
bling with both household and more unfamiliar wares.
The floor area was stacked neatly with wooden crates of
fruit and vegetables, to which customers served themselves ready for weighing. The wooden counter was
barely visible, its surface laden with packets, tins and
large, glass jars filled with coloured sweets. Archie
couldn't take it all in: advertising signs, tinned goods, an
absolute kaleidoscope of colours and so many smells.
Only one clear space was left in the centre for the large
brass weighing scales, a huge ornate brass till and its
operator, Rose Pollair, the owner of Porthmoor Stores.
Rose was, like her name, rosy-round-faced, with lipstick

pink lips, blonde hair tied up in a flowery headscarf, buxom-bodied in a flowery dress.

Mr Pollair, Rose's husband, was in the rear storeroom, shouting at the store's cat, Winston: 'You useless scabby, lazy, useless, overfed feline!'
Rose yelled a vociferous response over her shoulder to her husband in the back. 'Bob, don't you yell at my wonderful Winston, he's a bit shortsighted these days!'

'Rubbish!' came the disembodied reply. 'Nothing wrong with his eyesight; he's better fed than me, Rose!'

Rose laughed and directed her professional attention to a spectacularly tall, bean-like man with white trousers, white shirt, white cap. He was a vision in white except for the blue and white cravat tied at the throat, featuring an embroidered blue anchor. The cap he wore had a pseudo-naval officer badge on the peak. Once Archie had rudely gawked at him for a full minute, he turned his attention to the floor and Archie started staring again: he had the biggest feet he'd ever seen, in black patent winkle-pickers. As Rose started serving him, Archie had an opportunity to scrutinise his face: silver grey hair peeking out from under the cap, silver grey goatee beard, silver grey eyebrows. It was not however a naval look, more fancy dress, or perhaps a mad doctor in a laboratory or an escaped maniac! As Archie stared, a small wasp left a nearby fruit box and landed on the sleeve of the man's shirt; frantically, he brushed the wasp away and gave a grimace as he did so, smoothing down the shirt sleeve and brushing his white trousers for good measure, peering around for future invasions.

'Anything else, Mr De Quincey?' Rose enquired.

'Oh yes, some rope, if you have some.' 'Sorry, my dear, but you'll need to go to the Chandler's on the quay for that. After all, Mr De Quincey, it wouldn't be done for me to tread on Ted Hucknell's toes, if you know what I mean, or else Ted will be selling Ovaltine and Surf washing powder before you know it!' Rose winked conspiratorially at Archie.

The man gathered up his goods into a large cotton bag and handed Rose a new £5 note. 'Oh, nothing smaller, my dear?' Mr De Quincey pulled out a leather purse from his pocket and produced two crisp new £1 notes. Rose pushed the keys down on her ancient till, as it gave a shrill ring and the drawer shot out. Deftly avoiding it, she scooped out a ten shilling note and some loose change, closing the till drawer with a determined clunk, to hand the strange man his change. As he hurriedly left the shop, his eyes met Archie's and Archie felt the hairs go up on the back of his neck, like a chill wind suddenly coming through the store's door.

Rose picked up her tea cup as the door closed and re-marked, 'What an odd one, Archibald – but he is an artist and he is foreign!'

Archie took a deep breath and sighed, 'Does everyone know my name!'

'Oh yes, Archibald. Is it more paper you're wanting, or are you considering the aniseed twist sweets in my jar here, or is it a Jamboree Bag?' Archie loved sucking sweets, which he was not allowed, and a Jamboree Bag was a wasteful way to spend his money: a lurid green paper bag with some sweets, a toy and a small lolly. What it had to do with Scouts, Archie didn't know. Oh, but those tall glass jars full of coloured sweets, a veritable rainbow of colours! Archie looked around the shelves of tins, packets, bottles, cans. There were candles, torches, Christmas decorations, brown paper, scissors, babies' plastic rattles and wound on a thick piece of cardboard, ribbons. All at once Archie felt a sadness come over him. He turned his attention away from them and said, 'I'll have two ounces of aniseed twists, a tin of sardines and some sandpaper, please.'

'Well, Archibald, that's a fine mix. Sardines for Henry?'

'Shrew bait', he replied. He popped an aniseed twist into his mouth, saying 'Thank you' and left the Porthmoor Stores with a project or two in mind for the afternoon.

As he passed Pawley's Bakers, Lottie came out, resplendent in white apron and flour- sprinkled plimsolls. 'Oh Archie, it's a really low tide tomorrow, let's meet up after lunch at Pasty Cove, so bring a bucket and some rope.' With that, Lottie was gone, leaving a lovely smell of fresh bread filling the air behind her.

Time for a late lunch, or an early tea, either would be good. Clipping the cobblestones, Archie threaded through two families chatting in the sunshine and made his way back to Lighthouse Lookout Cottage, sucking thoughtfully on the aniseed twist. What would he need a rope and a bucket for?

CHAPTER 11
Henry's Plan, Corned Beef Fritters and Just Desserts

Archie arrived back at the cottage in time for a late lunch of crusty bread with butter and cheese from Moors Farm and pickled onions, as Hettie pickled her own shallots. The weather was good, so Hettie and Archie had lunch in the garden.

Hettie had to go out to see Rev. Wyatt and Judith, his wife, to discuss the Island Fete that was happening in a couple of weeks, and do her flower arranging spot in St Mawdate's Church. She usually dusted and gave the pews a polish, which Hettie believed made it easier to slip forward onto the hassocks for individual prayer. This was not a popular notion, as last month one of the Trott children shot forward too enthusiastically and hit his head on the pew in front. He really yelled, which in some ways was a blessing in disguise as the Reverend had to cut his sermon short that Sunday.

Actually, all the children liked to shuffle their bottoms on the polished seats, which was a keen distraction during the sermon or the notices. Once 'knees down for prayer' started, the parishioners at the back were most watchful due to an active ants' nest that seemed to invade every Sunday. Folk at the back of the church prayed for spiders, as these could be flicked away, whereas the ants had a tendency to crawl up your legs. The boys in the choir stalls were paid a handsome sixpence on Sunday for Mattins and a shilling for weddings. The boys had developed and nurtured a competitive spider-flicking operation during devotional prayer; if the floor was devoid of spiders, they pinched each other's calves, then had to endure the pain in silence, or lose their sixpence!

Flower arranging was a more serious matter and was also highly competitive. Hettie took a special interest in finding highly scented blooms, hoping the occupants of the front pews might not sneeze or worse, misaligning a bloom or displacing a herb or weed, which would be most upsetting to the front pews as they would focus on it for the whole of the sermon. One Christmas Hettie had added a few lit candles to her arrangement, but not only did they singe the holly foliage and create a stink, but the Reverend's Holy Communion linen cup cover caught alight and he had to rush out to the vestry with it aflame, with very un- church-like utterances. The Florist Arranging Group tried to ban Hettie, but the Reverend took into account the other church duties that Hettie undertook, which included the upcoming Island Fete which Hettie had been doing for years, and this was after all a financial mainstay for church repairs each year.

Left alone, Archie opened his tin of sardines into a dish from the dresser and sat still, waiting for the shrew to appear. Things did not go to plan, for whilst the shrew did not appear, Henry did. But after a few minutes the shrew did pop its head out from under the dresser. Henry flew at the dresser base, hissing wildly. The shrew did not return, and meanwhile Henry advanced towards the sardines and swiftly demolished the lot in a few mouthfuls, licking the plate clean. Archie was not impressed; Henry on the other hand sat by Archie's legs, purring and wiping the last of the sardine sauce on to Archie's bare legs. So much for that plan!

Archie retired to the garden with his paper and pencils, Henry dutifully following his 'snack pal'. As Henry settled down on a suitable clump of buttercups in his usual coiled position, licked and then slept, Archie sat on the pew and sketched him.

When Hettie returned, she asked Archie to go along the heather path and pick some fennel. Archie, once again asked, 'How will I recognise it, Great Aunt?' 'Why, Archibald, it's a tall plant with long stalks and yellow flowers, and when you crush the fern-like foliage between your fingers, it smells like aniseed twists from the sweetshop.'

Archie strolled out and soon found the tall plant. Crushing its feathery fronds between his hands, he breathed in the aroma. Amazed and overcome by it, he cut some with his penknife, and couldn't stop smelling the powerful scent. He closed his eyes and inhaled deeply, creating a kind of an internal photograph, so that he would retain the scent forever.

When Archie returned, Hettie was making corned beef fritters for tea. She had picked the beans earlier, but now engaged Archie in chopping the fennel stems finely, and then added them to mashed potatoes with lots of butter. The result was surprisingly tasty, and Archie demolished his tea.

'Great Aunt, do you use a lot of weeds for your cooking? Is this a tradition on Teal?'

'Archibald, getting anything for nowt on Teal is more than tradition, it's a way of life. This island has known harsh times, when we've had to adapt in order to survive. You waste nothing: everything foreign has to come by ship, boat or plane. We don't manufacture basins or metal here, so if we can find a few things like fresh herbs, salvaging from the land, or even the sea, it offsets the loss.'

Archie considered this, drinking a glass of home-made ginger beer, then completely changed the subject, approaching his Great Aunt for some assistance. 'Great Aunt, I've been told to bring a bucket and some rope for tomorrow. What on earth will they be for, beach games?'

Hettie concealed a wry smile. 'Oh Archibald, I believe you may be doing a little 'salvaging' of sorts tomorrow. I'll pack you up some biscuits and a thermos of hot cocoa to take with you, in case you get cold.'

Archie looked bemused and none the wiser. Beach Tiddly Winks, perhaps? As he was helping to clear the supper things, Hettie noticed the sketchbook she had bought him, open on the table. She could see a sketch Archie had made earlier when she was in her vegetable garden, tending her beans.

'Archibald, these are very good, I certainly didn't realise I had such an attractive bottom!' She studied the sketch. 'You have a real gift, you know. Not everyone has that gift; you could take it further, as a professional.'

Archie looked downcast at the sketch. Without looking up, he muttered, 'Tell my father, he thinks that art is 'doodling', it will never earn me a living, only proper school work will. When I return, he's arranged extra tuition for my maths.' Archie looked up at his Great Aunt imploringly. 'Great Aunt, I'm useless at maths, I hate it. He tells me that all I need is practice, that's all, more hard work and effort, that's all that's needed. To be honest, he thinks I'm an idiot, a lazy idiot who wants to doodle and daydream. He won't listen to me, ever!' With that, Archie got up sulkily, snatching up his sketchbook, leaving his Great Aunt concerned and alone in the kitchen.

Archie climbed the stairs to his bedroom. He sat on his bed, picked up a pencil and drew a picture of his father on top of a volcano with flames licking at his bottom, a pained look on his face, with bolts of lightning showering down on him, a lava stream of maths books slithering down the side of the volcano to a deep lake of sharks below. With some satisfaction, he tore off the sketch, screwed it up and threw it in the waste basket.

CHAPTER 12
A Carrot, Some Rope and Archie gets wet!

Archie spent a happy morning at the cottage. After a bowl of porridge, made to his Great Aunt's recipe: hot water, not milk, a knob of butter in the bottom of the bowl, a pinch of salt, and once his bowl was filled, a pool of milk around the edge, then, a generous sprinkling of sugar. It was smashing, and Archie's lips were sticking together. With pleasure.

Archie was in his bedroom after breakfast, brushing the cat fur off his eiderdown, as Henry had become very attached to him at night. Archie was a little sceptical about this attachment: he felt Henry looked on him as a secret food supply, and obviously Henry felt very warm on his bed. Hettie bustled in and suggested Archie try his hand at carving the piece of driftwood that William Duffie had given him. She asked him to follow her out to the garden and handed him a carrot!

Hettie showed Archie three basic cuts for carving, practising on the carrot first, to avoid primary injuries. She sat down on the pew and explained how to begin carving. She showed Archie how to cut towards your thumb, holding the carrot with the other thumb, then gently carve it in the same direction. Archie did this, carrot shavings littering the grass. Then Hettie explained a different cut, where Archie pushed away from the thumb, holding the carrot with the other thumb, pushing the carrot shavings upwards. Finally, she showed Archie how to use the blade to make a V cut at an angle into the carrot, then complete a matching V from below, forming a deep niche into the carrot.

Archie looked at his Great Aunt, impressed. 'Where did you learn that?' he exclaimed, carving the poor carrot to extinction. 'Well, Archibald, your Great Uncle Albert showed me. He once said that with all the driftwood on the beach and long stormy nights alone, it could prove more useful than embroidery!' Hettie handed Archie his driftwood and said seriously, 'Archibald, take your time, we don't want our budding artist thumbless before he becomes famous!' Archie blushed but was elated at what he could fashion. What would he try?

After lunch, and after Archie had cleared up all the carrot shavings from the grass (not ideal for the song thrush's diet), Archie followed Hettie out to a lean-to stone shed with a zinc roof. Looking inside, it was a jumble of garden spades, forks, sieves, broken candle sticks, handleless jugs and teapots, sacks, rusting tins and paraphernalia that had once served a purpose but now just gathered cobwebs. Hettie eventually located a bucket and unhooked a coil of rope from a nail on the wall, neatly tied and in surprisingly good order, and handed them to Archie.

'Archibald,' she spoke with some seriousness, 'make sure you return that rope as you were given it. Rope is a valuable item on Teal, so don't lose it!' Archie was somewhat confused: rope, a valuable item? Who knew!

He picked up the flask and biscuits as well, making his way through the High Street, closed today and quiet, as it was Sunday. No planes, no boats, no shops; Sunday closing day. Archie had been given permission to miss Mattins, but he would be going to Evensong later this evening with Great Aunt Hettie, wearing a clean shirt and trousers too, even his school jacket, but a good job his school cap had blown away!

Archie could hear Lottie and Ed at Pasty Cove as he made his way through the sand dunes and sea grass. Nelson was jumping about excitedly, pestering both friends in their wellington boots. They were pretending to joust with what looked like two giant butterfly nets. Archie deposited his flask and biscuits, proceeding slowly towards them. As he approached, they explained that they would be shrimping this afternoon.

Archie looked terrified, he did not 'do' water, this did not look like something he would enjoy. His face grew white and he started shaking his head. 'No, Lottie, I can't go fishing, it's deep out there, I'll probably drown!' Feeling slightly sick, he began to retreat to the sand dunes.

Lottie pursued him, 'Come on, Archie, you won't drown, you landlubber, and if you wear my wellies you won't even get your feet wet. Come on, we'll tie the bucket round your waist with the rope and you can stay in the shallows. Come on, Archibald, it's a new experience, you've nothing to fear but fear itself!' Lottie took hold of Archie's hand, told him to take off his sandals and led him gently back to the water's edge. She slipped off her wellingtons and passed them to him. She was wearing shorts and an old shirt. Once Archie had put the wellingtons on, Lottie tied the rope around Archie's waist and attached the other end to the bucket handle, which she had put in his hand. 'Don't drop the bucket, Archie, or we'll have no tea!'

Archie edged nervously towards the shallows, thinking of sharks, plodding very inelegantly through the wet sand, as if he had cement in each boot. He was not used to recreational pursuits; he looked rather like a cast member in an amateur pantomime, especially holding onto the bucket like grim death. Lottie skipped into the shallows, barefoot, holding her net aloft but looking back regularly to Archie. Nelson was further out, paddling in deeper water. As the tide flowed inwards towards the beach, the little rock pools started filling gradually, then spilling out to become warm shallow water. Archie watched his two friends, terrified they would go underwater and he would lose them too! Archie chewed his lips with concern, without noticing that the warm shallow water was slipping over the toes of his wellingtons.

He watched Lottie and Ed as they apparently 'hoovered' the shallows with their nets, under where the seaweed floated in clumps, like deep green tentacles, waving from the rocks they were attached to. Lottie pulled up her net, shook it and yelled to Archie in the shallows, 'Stand by, shipmate, shrimps coming aboard!'

As she reached him, she told him to put some seawater in the bucket. Archie reached down to scoop up some water and part-filled the bucket, his sleeves now wringing wet. Lottie up-ended the net, which had a smaller pocket in the end to trap the shrimps, and pushed out a number of colourless, wriggling, whiskery things into the bucket, where they continued swimming.

'Look, Archie,' she laughed, 'shrimpies for our tea!' Ed was wading back through the rising water, his shorts were wet, his net equally full of these things. Ed turned them out into Archie's bucket, with the bonus of a small crab and a nasty-looking spiky fish. He carefully hooked these out and threw them back into the shallows. Ed and Lottie made numerous forays to the deeper waters, and before long Archie's bucket held a large number of jumping whiskery shrimps. He gingerly put his hand in, and one nipped him. Archie yelled. Lottie immediately yelled back, 'Don't drop that bucket, Archie!'

Archie didn't see the water rising, and before he knew it Lottie, Ed and Nelson were quite near him. His bucket was now quite busy with all these transparent leaping shrimps. A small punt that was on the sand earlier was now afloat and the water was up to the top of Archie's wellies. The bucket was becoming very heavy and Archie's arms ached from holding onto the bucket. It held a few random extra creatures co-habiting with the shrimps, having been hijacked along with them.

When they all returned to the beach, Archie hadn't realised that Lottie's wellies were full of water and his shorts were wet. They all splashed and waded back to the beach, too wet to care. Archie and Ed removed their wellies, poured out the water in them and placed the bucket, now disconnected from the rope, in the shade. The trio found a large flat rock to sit on, and Archie retrieved his flask of hot cocoa and pack of biscuits from the sand dunes where he had left them. He unscrewed the flask and poured out enough for them all. They all had their snacks, and Ed's mother had provided extra cups and packs of Smith's crisps, with little blue bags of salt in the bag. Of course, it was Lottie who produced the star of the show: lemon curd tarts. What a feast they had!

'Well, Archie,' Lottie munched as she spoke, 'how was your first shrimping expedition?'

Archie laughed. 'Those little monsters bite, don't they? And I'm so, so wet!'

Ed munched one of Hettie's oatmeal biscuits and remarked to Archie, 'They won't be biting soon. We'll take these to my dad's shed on the quay and cook them on his primus stove.'

CHAPTER 13
Something Fishy Cooking on Teal Island

The threesome slowly made their way down to Ed's dad's fishing shed on the quay, holding nets aloft and taking turns to hold the heavy bucket. The bucket was full, and to Archie's horror a few shrimps tried to escape their fate on their route to the cooking pot. Archie carefully picked them up, whiskery, leggy, nipping, and transferred them back to the bucket.

The Trevithick fishing shed was one of many on the quayside: granite-built, zinc-roofed and entered through two blue wooden doors, badly in need of some redecorating. Once inside, despite the windows, it was a dark stinky building: wooden shelves of ropes, metal tools, the floor piled high with tiers of beehive-shaped willow-woven crab baskets. There were several zinc baths, a long wooden bench, many boots, fisherman's smocks, dungarees and hats for all seasons. In one corner, on the wooden bench, there was a primus stove, several stained and chipped cups and various canisters marked as 'Tea',

'Coffee', 'Sugar' and one marked 'Not for Nelson!'
Archie prised open the lid: oh, custard cream biscuits!

Ed searched for a large handleless aluminium saucepan
which he filled with seawater from the harbour. He then
lit the primus, with matches kept in an '*Old Holborn*'
tobacco tin, and waited for the water to boil. He asked
Archie and Lottie to help him lift the bucket and transferred the shrimps, now frantically diving to their doom
in the boiling sea-water. Archie felt it was quite sad, and
his lips quivered as the bounty of whiskered transparent
shrimps fell still and as if by magic turned pink. Ed saw
the look, and lifting Archie's mood began to expound,
'Did you know, Archie, that shrimps have their skeleton
on the outside and those pointy noses are for stabbing
enemies?' Archie looked surprised. 'Do you mean to say
that those poor pink shrimps actually stabbed me?'

Lottie looked upwards, tutting. 'Don't encourage him,
Archie.'

Ed, refusing to be silenced, continued, 'And they talk to
each other in the water, making clicking noises.'

Lottie looked at Archie, as Ed scooped out the pink
shrimps, now very still and very cooked. She winked
conspiratorially at Archie and started making clicking
noises with her tongue. Archie joined in loudly and the
pair pretended to swim like shrimps, then fall dramatic-
ally to the floor, deceased.

'Very funny, you two,' giggled Ed. 'One day you'll thank
me for this knowledge, when I'm a famous journalist.'

The mood suddenly changed. A well-built man in a plaid
shirt, blue dungarees and wellingtons stood in the doorway, his bulk blocking the daylight from the shed. His

face was wrinkled, weathered, a mop of brown, curly, wiry hair just protruding from under a blue woolly hat. The eyes seared into Ed's as he barked to all three: 'Journalist, eh? Is that while you're hauling out the crab pots, or picking the crab after it's cooked?' Ed's face dropped, eyes downcast. The man, who was obviously Ed's father, continued, 'No time for day-dreaming, boy. They won't put food on the table or clothes on your back!'

Ed turned towards the shrimps, just wishing he could have jumped into the pot with them. Lottie sensed the mood was dark and skilfully interjected, 'Good day, Mr Trevethick, this is Archie.'

Samuel Trevethick studied Archie for a moment and said, 'Ah, yes, the Bosworth lad; your parents fallen down a volcano yet?'

Archie couldn't help thinking Mr Trevethick had read his thoughts after his outburst, and replied without hesitation, 'Not that I know of, but I haven't heard from them in Guatemala, so one never knows.'

Samuel Trevethick eyed the boy suspiciously. Archie couldn't help being a little rude, for he felt his new-found friend was being knocked down by his father. Ed was, he believed, a clever lad and did not fit the profile of a crab fisherman. Samuel Trevethick was not in a good mood: he ignored the three friends and sought out a fuel can from under the bench. Turning to the three, he informed them in heated terms, 'Some rotten thief has taken fuel from my boat and George Trott's. It's despicable. I was out running an errand for Reverend Wyatt when I ran out of fuel. I knew I had plenty for Monday's crab pots. I never leave my boat without fuel. William

Duffie came to my rescue, but who would do such a thing! You three keep your eyes open. It's scandalous!'

Ed raised an eyebrow, sensing a story in the making. 'Dad, could it be the teenagers from Norwhel?'

'No lad, why would they use fuel to come here to steal fuel? George Trott is furious, and so am I. Ed, get those shrimps in the cool, lad, you don't want them to be spoiled; and clean up the saucepan. Remember, tomorrow morning it's your turn to help your mother crab pick.'

Samuel Trevethick pulled his hat down, covering his bushy brown eyebrows. His blue-grey eyes had a coldness to them, but when he turned to Lottie he softened: 'You see, Lottie, you know how if I run out of fuel and the sea condition deteriorates, or the fog comes in, it could be dangerous if the boat drifts. I could finish up in a strong current outside the islands and be done for!'

Lottie nodded in agreement, then reached into her shoulder bag and fished out a lemon curd tart that she had planned to give to Archie; but she held it out to Mr Trevethick as a peace offering, hoping to calm his temper before he got home. Samuel Trevethick took the tart, sniffed it, smiled and put the whole tart in his mouth in one go. They all laughed. Lottie then took down three small enamel bowls from the shelves, dusted them off and shared out the shrimps, before the trio made their way back from the quay to their respective households.

Archie stank of fish and all his wet clothes were sticking to him. Time to clean up for church, or perhaps the congregation would dispel if he went in as he was! He carried the shrimps in one hand, the bucket containing the

64

flask and the neatly coiled length of rope in the other. Tea time!

CHAPTER 14
Gossip, Suspicions and Flying Underpants

Hettie was snoozing in her chair in the kitchen when Archie, dripping wet, returned to the cottage. Henry was curled up on Hettie's lap, but the first sniff of shrimps sent Henry leaping off Hettie's skirt to wrap himself around Archie's damp legs.

'Fresh gossip, Great Aunt!' Archie yelled as he came through the door.

Hettie told Archie to change into dry things for church, then took the bucket, flask, neatly coiled rope in one hand and the enamel bowl of shrimps in the other. Henry followed the enamel bowl of shrimps, from Archie's hand to Hettie's hand to the kitchen table.

Archie returned wearing dry clothes; Hettie put his wet things on Agatha's rail, always toasty warm, and Archie stood with his back to the Aga, warming his bottom nicely. Hettie sat down at the kitchen table to shell the shrimps; these were not big shrimps and it was a fiddly process. Archie sat opposite her and they shelled together. Archie, in a privileged gossiping position, couldn't wait to tell Hettie about the fuel thefts in the harbour. Hettie was 'all attention'; she even chose to ignore Archie feeding Henry a shrimp under the table, she was so anxious for new gossip.

'It's a disgrace, Archie!' she spluttered, for all boating problems were of the greatest importance in an island community. Hettie made a mental note to call Mavis Pentworth, the island post lady, in the morning. 'Mind you, Archie, there are a few folk that I reckon could sink that low; folks here have long memories. We get along, as you have to on a small island, but we don't forget. For instance, you wouldn't see me sitting next to Deloris Devonport at the old folks' Christmas lunch. She's weird, goes around at night with a torch on her head and waving a shrimping net looking for flying bugs; she's some sort of escapologist!'

Archie hid a grin. 'Do you mean an entomologist, Great Aunt?'

'Yes, Archibald, that's the gist of it, some sort of . . . 'ologist!'

'So,' continued Archie, 'do you think she took the fuel?'

'Oh no, Archibald, I just don't like her. She once sold my best hat at the island jumble sale.'

'Did you donate it to the jumble sale?'

'No, the idiot woman! I took it off to try on a cardigan, and she sold it!'

Archie decided to return to the subject in hand: 'So who do you think could do this? Ed's father was furious.'

'Well Archibald,' Hettie said, popping a shrimp in her mouth, adding a splash of salad cream to the rest of the shelled shrimps in the bowl and mixing them together while Archie contemplated that these poor shrimps had been stripped of their exoskeleton, 'it has to be someone with a boat, stands to reason, and they had to have a punt to get to the boats in the harbour. Then they had to have a fuel can and a piece of pipe to get the fuel out of the fuel tank and into the can. But who would need fuel for their boat? It's a mystery, Archibald!' Hettie put the shrimp and salad cream mixture between two slices of buttered bread and made a sandwich for them, which she cut in half. Archie slipped Henry a few more undressed shrimps under the table, then chomped on his sandwich, licking the corners of his mouth.

'Ah,' concluded Hettie, 'it could well be Captain Wilber-force. Mavis doesn't think he's a captain at all, because he had a letter arrived last month addressed to Harold White, and he's a captain who doesn't have a boat; that's another odd thing.'

Archie finished his shrimp sandwich and pondered on a captain without a boat: certainly highly suspicious. There was a silence between them, and then the parrot started squawking again: 'Idiota! Idiota!' Archie rushed out to the kitchen lean-to and bent close to Captain Cook. 'Try saying something nice, you bad bird, try Archie, Archie!'

The bird was now too close for comfort and it was too great a temptation: the parrot opened his beak and nipped Archie sharply on the nose. 'Ouch! Ouch!' Archie hopped from one foot to the other and yelled, 'You flea-bitten mass of cushion feathers, you, you, your mother was a mattress!'

Captain Cook hopped from one end of his perch to the other, opened his wings and swooped around the room squawking. He settled on the wicker laundry basket, stared at Archie, then picked up a pair of Archies under-pants in his beak, opened his wings once more and flew outside, through the open lean-to door. The parrot was

flying very determinedly, in the direction of the Pawleys'
cottage, Moors View and...Lottie!

CHAPTER 15
Storms and Shouts

Archie was distracted during evensong, thinking about the fuel thefts. It was during the notices about the forthcoming Island Fete that Archie's mind really wandered. Reverend Wyatt concluded his information with, 'Just take a moment to look at the poster in Porthmoor Stores to see if you can help or donate.' It was the mention of Porthmoor Stores that made Archie remember Mr De Quincey asking for rope. Why would an artist need rope? Archie decided he would call on Lottie and Ed tomorrow to see if they had any ideas. Archie must have looked as if he was really concentrating on the Reverend's service, for when he shook Archie's hand enthusiastically afterwards, pumping it up and down relentlessly, he said, 'So good to see young people attentive in the service, Archibald.' Archie then even wondered if the Reverend had a boat. He wasn't the stereotypical reverend: he was very young, sort of 'Rock n Roll', his nose furnished with an unusual quantity of nasal hair; and for added measure of interest, when his wife shook Archie's hand, there was what Archie perceived as a noticeable waft of alcohol on her breath as she spoke (though it could have been mouth wash). There was also something very superficial about their enthusiasm. Archie was making mental notes on suspicious characters who could fit the profile of a fuel thief.

As they left St Mawdate's Anglican Church, the sky was a threatening grey and the wind was beginning to gust. Hettie hung onto Archie's arm as they passed the harbour. The boats whilst shackled to their buoys, rose up and down on the white-crested waves. The wind gusted and howled through the buildings and fairly blew the pair along the cobblestones, down the sandy scrub track, now blinding them both with the sand blowing in their eyes, the hedges bending and waving like crazy figures in the landscape, in danger of becoming disembodied; with a little more wind, they might even uproot and dance away independently.

At last they pushed the cottage door shut behind them, and all was suddenly quiet and warm. Archie found it hard to believe that the weather could turn so quickly. Hettie turned on the lamps and began heating a thick vegetable soup on the Aga. In no time they were sitting down to eat, crusty bread dipped in the hot soup, relishing the warmth of the kitchen while the storm raged outside. Suddenly they were startled by a loud explosion, not close by but in the distance, somewhere in the direction of Norwhel.

Archie rushed to the window in time to see a great burst of light in the darkened sky. 'Fireworks, Great Aunt?' he asked, his nose pressed against the window, looking for further activity.

Hettie looked worried. 'No, lad, it's a '*shout*': that boom and the light in the sky is the Norwhel lifeboat maroon being fired off, calling the lifeboat men to the lifeboat slip to launch the lifeboat. There must be some poor devil in trouble at sea, and on a night like this, it's scary for both sailor and lifeboat men: they risk their lives every time. But Archibald, that's the way it's always been on the islands: since the first sailing ships got into trouble on the rocks around here, the island men have gone out to rescue them."

Archie could sense his Great Aunt's concern. 'Wouldn't the lighthouse have warned the sailors about the rocks?' he questioned.

'That doesn't help, Archibald, if a mast breaks, or an engine fails. In a storm like this, with a boat or ship out of control, huge waves could send even the biggest boat onto the rocks. The sea is a dangerous place, Archibald. The moment you disrespect it, it will consume you.'

Archie shuddered at the thought of the weather outside: the howling, lashing wind and now torrents of rain. He thought of a crew of brave men launching a lifeboat to rescue some poor sailor or sailors in distress. Archie put on his mackintosh and ventured past the sleeping cat into the back garden, to experience in some little way what the lifeboat men were coping with. He could barely stand up: branches were being strewn everywhere and the rain was driving down and hurting his face, taking his breath away.

It was at this precise moment, as Archie stood almost inviting the weather to do its worst, that he decided he would make a stand. He must face his fears, he must. He turned away towards the cottage: a contrast to the boy who had arrived on Teal. Once back inside, Archie towelled his hair dry, hung up his mackintosh and got ready for bed. He curled up in the front room of the cottage, deep in a huge comfy armchair, sipping his mug of Ovaltine.

Hettie was awaiting a call from one of the boatmen, and looked pensive as she spoke to Archie: 'The thing is, Archie, these lifeboat men are and always have been volunteers; they are brothers, fathers on the islands, they are our family. These Atlantic waters are deadly, but many of the boatmen don't learn to swim. They reckon that once you're in the water, there's nowhere to swim to and no time to survive. These temperatures could plunge a body into hypothermia in as little as twenty minutes; just that icy water splashing in your face constantly. The lifejackets worn by the lifeboat crew might not save you if you were in the water for some time.'

When the telephone rang, Hettie sat up, listening intently to the caller with her eyes closed. Then, after a few minutes of conversation, during which Archie leant forward impatiently in his chair, he saw Hettie become visibly relaxed and a smile spread across her face. She bid the caller goodnight and thank you, put the receiver down and sighed deeply.
'So?' Archie asked. 'Well, Great Aunt, were they rescued? What happened?'

Hettie picked up her cup of Ovaltine and sighed again. 'A yacht had broken its mast in these winds and was drifting with the current away from the islands.'

'What happened?' Archie asked, putting his drained mug down.

'Well, the lads launched really quickly and found them in time. Edward's father, Samuel Trevethick, got a rope onto the bow of the yacht; he had to jump from the bow of the lifeboat across to the bow of the yacht. The swell of the sea was something terrible, and it must have been terrifying trying to gauge the rise and fall of each wave and judging when was the right time to jump. So dangerous; he could have slipped between the two boats and been crushed. He secured the rope so that the yacht was now attached to the lifeboat, ready to tow. It was a close thing: six souls on the yacht, four men, a woman and a lad of twelve. All safe! They are in Norwhel harbour now, the yacht secured against the harbour wall, awaiting repair. The people on the yacht are, as we speak, eating supper and being found beds for the night.'

Archie began to realise later, as he tucked himself under his blankets and watched the lighthouse beam bidding sleep, that these islands were not just places for beach-combing and coves to play in. The sea was an unpredict-able force that could turn from warm shallows to grey troughs of wild waves very quickly. Ed must have been so scared for his father tonight, all differences between them forgotten, as the lifeboat launched.

Hettie tucked him in and said, 'No worry, Archibald, sleep safe tonight. William Duffie keeps a watch out: he spotted the yacht in distress and signalled to Norwhel.' She leant over Archie and kissed him on the forehead, looking towards the lighthouse beam and saying, 'Well done, William, good night!'

CHAPTER 16
Archie Becomes a Baker and Gets Creative

Hettie had errands to run and gossip to distribute, so she left the cottage early, after giving Archie tea and a huge bowl of porridge. He drank his tea and cleared most of his porridge. Henry licked up the remnants and lay near the Aga to sleep.

Archie deliberated over his list of suspects, and looking out of the cottage window was surprised to see that the weather had changed once more. No longer grey sky and raining, but a blue sky with white clouds scudding by at high speed; a day for an extra layer of clothing. In a drawer in the bedroom he found a thick sweater of questionable provenance: Great Uncle Albert's, Archie suspected, smelling of mothballs. It was so big it almost drowned him, but as Archie opened the cottage door he was glad of it.

Henry opened one eye as the door closed and considered the choice of dozing or annoying Captain Cook. The troublesome bird had returned after his morning exercise around the island, carrying a child's vest in his beak. Hettie had thrust it hurriedly in her shopping basket, to deposit it in the lost property box in the Island Hall. She was ashamed of the wretched bird's habits and tried to disassociate herself from Captain Cook's criminal shopping expeditions. Never a crab or a fish, even a piece of fruit or a vegetable, but personal items like one sock, a vest, even one of Macey Trott's ample-sized brassieres! He was a disgrace; she should have plucked and cooked him long ago, except last month he had scooped up Deloris Davenport's head torch, so that the wretched woman had to delay her nocturnal bug hunting for a month until a replacement arrived. Shame the bird had never brought her misappropriated hat back! While Hettie made her way to meet Mavis at the Post Office sorting office, Archie had to don odd socks as one of his favourite pair had disappeared. He left the cottage, battling against the wind, and made his way to the High Street. Following the smell of baking, he popped his head around the back door of Pawley's Bakery. Lottie was in the kitchen, dressed in her white apron and white plimsolls, her red hair tied back with a white headscarf. She was standing in front of a huge wooden table covered with lots of white pastry circles ready for the morning's pasty making. The kitchen door was divided: the top half swung open while the bottom half stayed shut. Archie leaned in, while Lottie beckoned to Archie to come into the kitchen. He undid the bottom latch and went in, locking the bottom part behind him. It was toasty warm after the cold wind outside.

'What were you saying, Lottie? I couldn't hear you out in the wind.'

Lottie took one look at Archie's giant-sized Arran-styled jumper and giggled. 'Archie, it's your lucky morning; take that enormous jumper off and put this on.' She handed Archie a large white apron and assumed command, fastening the apron ties behind his back and telling him to wash his hands at the corner sink. Lottie had a younger brother, Samson, who always had disgusting hands; all boys had nasty fingernails. 'Right Archie,' she ordered, 'time to learn a new skill.'

Archie groaned. 'Not another new experience! I'm not killing cows or handling their personal bits, am I. Lottie?'

'Archie, you are so, so vanilla. Watch me, look: swede, potatoes, onions and beef.' On the table were several bowls of raw ingredients and Archie watched Lottie as she took a small handful from each: yellow swede chunks, white potato chunks, chopped onions and red skirt beef pieces. Archie followed Lottie round the table, putting a spoonful of each in the middle of each circle of pastry. There followed a sprinkle of salt and lastly some flour.

As Archie held the flour bowl, Lottie took a handful and threw it over Archie's head. He squealed, then retaliated, throwing some back at her. Lottie screamed and jumped up and down, shaking her head.

It was this point in their antics that they heard Mrs Pawley's voice from the shop: 'How are those pasties coming along, Scarlett?' They both fell silent, stifling giggles.

Archie watched Lottie fold the pastry in half; he followed her, copying what she was doing, taking turns, until all the pasties were folded into semi-circles. Next was the tricky bit: Lottie crimped the edges until the pasty was sealed. Once they were all completed, she handed Archie a small knife, while she beat some egg yolks in a bowl. Archie gazed at the knife and at Lottie.

'Come on Archie', she laughed, 'pierce the pasty like it's someone you don't like!'

Archie held the small knife and with some abandon pierced each pasty. Lottie brushed some of the pasties with a little egg and then handed the bowl to Archie to finish the rest. She picked up a giant wooden, long-handled paddle to slide under each pasty and push them onto a baking tray. Archie enjoyed this 'painting' considerably, and was thoughtful as he brushed each pasty with a flourish of a wave pattern. He looked at the completed trays and said, 'Why is it, Lottie, that parents always look at what you can't do, rather than what you can?' Lottie looked directly at him as he raised his eyes to hers. 'Archie, my frustration is that I can do the things I'm supposed to do, and I do them well, but it isn't what I want to do; it isn't who I want to be.' With that, Lottie pulled on white oven gloves and slid the trays into the hot oven, banging the door firmly shut, then threw the oven gloves down on the table. '45-50 minutes, Archie, at 180 degrees centigrade. I could do this with my eyes shut; some days I try to do just that, so I can't see a future of aprons, ovens and superficial burns to my fingers!'

Once the table was wiped clean and they could smell the pasties cooking, Lottie quickly pulled on her hat and sweater. Archie pulled on his giant sweater and they prepared to leave the bakery kitchen, opening both parts of the stable door. Lottie yelled to her mother in the shop as they left, 'Pasties cooking, mum, the alarm's set, I'm off to Ed's.'

Mrs Pawley's voice responded from the shop, 'OK, Scarlett, be back later to help serve in the shop. I've got to see Mr Trott about some more skirt beef. Take a few sausage rolls for your lunches.'

'OK, mum!' Lottie yelled as she picked up a few sausage rolls from the morning's baking trays, packing them in greaseproof paper. 'Come on, Archie,' she said, linking their arms.

Archie flushed: another 'new experience' with a girl! To cover his blushes, he announced, 'Let's find Ed and talk suspicions!'

'Oh, by the way, Archie,' added Lottie, 'that wretched parrot flew into the back door of our cottage last night and dropped a pair of men's underpants on our kitchen table!' Archie went redder still and turned his head to look in a shop window. 'The funny thing was, Archie, he kept repeating some foreign word.' Archie looked at her thoughtfully, keen to change the subject from his underwear. 'Yes, it wasn't his usual squawking, it was distinctly not European. It sounded like 'Hoobyraysra! Hoobyraysra!'

Archie laughed. 'Perhaps it's some sort of secret love language! Love language and underpants!'

Lottie looked thoughtful, then when she saw Archie was grinning, she dug him hard in the ribs with her elbow, so he bent double as they passed the Post Office. Lottie marched ahead, calling, 'Come on, vanilla slow coach, I have to ask Ed a very personal favour.' She raised both eyebrows and winked.

CHAPTER 17
Picking Crab, Another Theft and Lottie Asks a Favour

Ed was working in his kitchen at Harbour View Cottage when Archie and Lottie arrived in high spirits. Like the bakery, the kitchen had a stable door, keeping both heat and fish smells to a minimum. Nelson was on sentry duty, guarding the kitchen door, tail wagging, ears twitching, licking his slobbery lips, no pretense of being a guard dog. He was rewarded with many pats, tickled tum and scratched ears. Nelson sat obediently, head on one side, looking at Lottie. He would not be disappointed today, for Lottie had a sausage roll for him. Lottie scoffed the pastry part, to keep Nelson slim, but what dog doesn't like a sausage? Having fed the sentry, Lottie pushed past him into the kitchen, where Nelson was not allowed; Ed's father said it was because of germs, though Ed maintained sarcastically that Nelson hadn't caught anything yet!

Ed was poised between a huge cauldron of boiling crabs and a marble work surface littered with dismembered crabs. The room was enveloped in a mist of fishy steam. Suddenly, appearing like a ghost in the midst of the steam, Dottie Trevethick approached the table with a deep wicker basket packed with very active, red shelled crabs, cartoon-like eyes on sticks, robotic moving clicking claws, clambering over each other and out of their basket prison. There would be no escape for them now.

Ed was not in a good mood: taking the cooked crabs from the steaming cauldron without ceremony or obvious compassion, he snapped off the legs and claws and pushed the body case of the crab out with his thumbs. This ritual was not done with dedication, and the crabs seemed to be getting the worst of Ed's mood. Lottie met Archie's eyes and said, 'Come on, Archie, apron on, wash your hands and prepare to autopsy these poor murdered crabs. If we don't help, Ed won't be free for some time.'

Archie was unfortunately transfixed with horror: the process of living and dying upset him visibly, and he desperately wanted to run away. Lottie met his gaze, took him by both shoulders and told him firmly, 'This is what friends do, Archie, they suffer claws, steam and stinky hair to escape for sausage rolls on Rocky Point.' Archie managed to pull himself together, fixed on Lottie's raised eyebrows and determined green-eyed stare.

Ed looked up as he snapped legs and claws and remarked, 'Archie, why are your eyebrows and ears covered in white stuff?' Archie rubbed his face quickly and replied, 'There was an explosion in the flour cupboard. Well, Lottie started it.'

Ed grinned and his mood began to change. 'Do you know, Archie, that crabs are decapods? That means they have ten feet, and the biggest Japanese spider crabs can grow up to 13 feet in length, twice my dad's height!'

Lottie groaned and covered her eyes. 'Ed, I think I prefer your silent moods.'

Archie decided he would encourage Ed and irritate Lottie. 'What do they eat, Ed, with all those legs and claws to fill?'

'Ah, an intelligent question, thank you for your interest, Archibald. They eat anything.' Ed looked quite mercilessly at Archie, with well-humoured eyes. 'Often dead fish!' 'Ugh' was the response. Archie wished he hadn't asked.

'Actually, Archie, crabs look fierce with those stalky eyes and those scary claws, but they have many enemies.' Lottie closed her eyes and kept thinking about the freshly baked sausage rolls. 'Oh yes,' Ed continued, not to be silenced, 'octopus, alligators, and even birds swoop down in the shallows of the sea for the smaller ones.'

Archie was genuinely interested. 'Come on, Ed, how would a bird catch a crab?'

Ed raised a cooked, deceased crab above the marble slab and theatrically dropped it with a resounding crack. 'Like a thrush with a snail, Archie: drop it, smash it, nosh it!'

Lottie was losing patience. 'Come on, lads, one process each. Ed, you take out the dead men's fingers, the poisonous bits. Archie, you pick out the brown meat, put it separately in that bowl. I'll break the body in two, then take out all the white meat with this metal pick.'

Having taken out the dead men's fingers, Ed moved swiftly to the legs, opening them and picking out the white meat. He then showed Archie how to crack the claws like Christmas nuts and pick out the white meat too. Archie, Lottie and Ed moved quickly, and Ed could smell the aroma of the sausage rolls.

Archie peered into the cauldron with its newest victims. 'Is it like shrimps, Ed, instant death?'

'Nope,' Ed replied animatedly, picking and depositing the white meat as he answered, 'about 15-18 or 20 minutes, depending on the weight of the crab.' Archie was intrigued. 'Do you do this with your mum every day, Ed?'

Ed looked down at the marble slab and smashed more legs with enthusiasm. 'Two hours a day, and I've just started going out with dad to hook up the buoy that marks the string of pots, then attaching a line to the pot as we drop the empty pot near the rocks, where crabs like to live. The next day dad heaves up the basket, full of crabs, we hope, on the gunwales of the boat; bringing the pot into the boat is hard work. We take the crabs out and drop the empty pot back into the sea to catch more crabs. The result of this operation, you see here. Furthermore, because I know Archie is interested, did you know that crabs can grow a claw back if they lose one?' This information was delivered without interest, as Ed already knew all this.

Surprisingly, Archie was interested; it was better than volcanoes. 'Why do they go in the baskets when they can eat stuff in the sea?'

'Ah well, Archie, my attentive crab student, we bait them with bits of mackerel. They crawl in the hole in the crab pot, rather like going into a cave through a crevice. However, they can get in but they can't get out.'

Lottie decided she would enter the conversation, hoping to end it. 'Yes, Archie, that's the sort of string of pearls you can see around the rocks: the coloured buoys bobbing on the surface, each pot attached to a rope. But tourists and other novice boat folk often run through the ropes attached to the buoys, and also to the pots. The rope gets tied up in their propellers, ruining their boat and the island's crab business.'

They finished picking the last of today's crabs, turned off the cauldron of hot water, cleaned down and took off their aprons, turning to more interesting conversation: fuel thefts! Archie told them both about Mr De Quincey and his suspicions. Ed was now full of enthusiasm and startled the other two by suggesting they all go snoop round De Quincey's cottage, and 'see if we can find any clues'.
Archie was horrified. 'Isn't that burglary?'

'No, Archie, only if we go in. But we should also consider any other suspicious characters.'

At this juncture, Ed's father appeared. Archie was a little starstruck by Mr Trevethick's presence, remembering his brave action on the lifeboat: 'Mr Trevethick, you must have been afraid, leaping from one boat to another in such a storm.'

Ed smiled. He was really proud of his father's lifeboat duties; it was just the crab fishing that held no glory or dedication for him.

Samuel Trevethick smiled at Archie. 'Archibald, if you live on a small island, you must be prepared to turn your hand to many things.'

'Have you ever fallen in, sir?' Archie enquired.

'Oh yes, lad, but I try not to make a habit of it! The thing is, Archie, the only way to tow a yacht in trouble is by putting a line onto the bow and cleating it on. I couldn't throw it across, as the sea was heaving. You judge it by the rise and fall of the sea and the rise and fall of the lifeboat. Rope, Archie, is the gold of the fisherman or men who work the ocean.' Archie nodded; he'd heard this from his Great Aunt. 'But remember, Archibald, undone or untidy, it will undo you; and if you run across it with a motor boat, it will foul your propeller, and then the boat is out of action. That's when you have to summon the lifeboat.' Suddenly, Samuel Trevethick frowned, his dark mood returning and related to the trio that last night a punt was taken from the harbour; the police were coming over from Norwhel tomorrow. 'This is a bad business. Is it a stranger or our own folk? I'm really worried.'

The trio walked away from Harbour View Cottage, all silently digesting the latest news, Nelson yapping at their heels. As they approached Rocky Point, their thoughts focused temporarily on the sausage rolls.

Lottie turned to Ed and with a somewhat cavalier and throwaway line said, 'Can I borrow some of your clothes for next week, Ed?'

Both boys stopped in their tracks and stared at her. Ed's eyes almost popped out of his head. 'Oh Lottie, what are you planning? Will we all have to play a part in this?'

Lottie marched ahead and looking back, tossing her red hair, said with a wicked grin as she turned on her heel, 'Oh boys, I hope so!'

Archie groaned. 'Oh no, not another new experience!'

CHAPTER 18
Archie Reaches New Heights and Suspicions are Raised.

After clambering over banks of heather and ever bigger granite rocks on the headland, accompanied by their 'sherpa' dog Nelson, the trio reached the top of Rocky Point. Puffing, they sat down on some flat rocks while Archie caught his breath and Nelson worried the sausage roll package. Archie gripped his chosen, secure rock with both hands, looking forward to a warm Lighthouse Lookout Cottage later.

Lottie went straight to the edge and looked down to Rocky Point beach below. Rocky Point beach was one of the few areas that walkers couldn't get access to: there was no path from the top to the beach below. The granite cliff was made up of vertical grey granite slabs, the only relief being clumps of purple flowering sea thrift and a few kittiwakes' nests. The beach below was mostly sand, with a few scattered rocks near the foot of the cliff, colourfully shrouded by sea kale. Boats could reach the beach at high tide, but once the tide fell, if they forgot the time, they would have to wait until the tide rose again to leave. There were also a number of pot buoys further out, which Ed's father used to mark his crab pots.

Lottie turned around, face flushed, and shouted to Archie, 'Come on, Archie, come and look.'

Archie stayed firm. 'Tempting, but no!'

'Oh come on, why are you so afraid of heights. Archie?' 'It's not the heights I'm afraid of, Lottie, it"s the falling that I'm not keen on. Come away from the edge, Lottie!'

Ed stood up and helped Archie to his feet. 'Come on, Archie. Lottie and I will hold you tight, you won't fall. Why come here and not see where you are?' Archie put his lips very tightly together and shook his head and sat down again.

Lottie came back to the pair and bent down, looking Archie in the eyes, and took him by the shoulders. 'Come on, son of volcano climbers, we promise to keep you safe. Look at me, Archie!' Ed and Lottie pulled Archie up and, holding tightly to an arm each, propelled Archie towards the edge. Archie had his eyes shut tight. 'For saints' sake, Archie, just one look, then sausage rolls,' humoured Lottie.

Archie opened his eyes and looked down, gripped firmly by Lottie and Ed. His eyes swooped down to the view below, like a telescope brought into focus. Suddenly, without warning, Archie's legs wobbled, he felt unsteady, he felt hot, he felt nauseous.

Lottie spoke calmly 'Focus, Archie. Where's the horizon?' Archie looked ahead and felt better, his nausea subsiding. 'Now look at the sea, Archie.' Archie looked at the sea and began feeling calmer. 'Now, Archie, look at the beach, not the cliff. Can you see the sea kale?' Archie concentrated and located the bank of kale below, so nodded his head.

'Now, Archie, let your eyes follow the kale upwards to the pink sea thrift, bringing your focus up to my face.' Archie looked in her eyes and his legs stopped wobbling. Archie felt calm. Lottie and Ed slowly released their grip. Archie stepped back a little and this time he looked directly ahead, avoiding the plunge down. Lottie patted Archie on the back. 'Now we can have our lunch. Well, Archibald Bosworth, another new experience; just the water to tackle.' Archie ignored the last comment and proceeded to the flat rocks where they had been sitting, pursued by a permanently peckish Nelson.

Ed, ever the educator, keen to impart pertinent information on the subject in hand, said, 'Do you know, my dad told me that some chap called Nicholas Alkinade, an RAF tail gunner, fell from a plane at 18,000 feet!' There was a suspended silence from Archie and Lottie as Ed helped himself to a sausage roll before continuing his latest bank of knowledge. 'No parachute; his fall was broken by trees and soft snow, amazing!'

Archie shook his head. 'Well, Ed, I''ll be sure to take a parachute with me on my next plane journey.' Lottie grinned and added, 'Or snow!'

Archie was beginning to feel more able as he sat down, reflecting on the changes taking place within him. Ed munched on his sausage roll and, without looking away from his lunch, asked Archie if he had always been afraid of heights. Archie, feeling fully recovered from his ordeal, helped himself to a sausage roll and gave a little of the sausage to Nelson who was waiting patiently at their collective feet. Archie took a bite and after a moment said, 'I lost my confidence a couple of years ago, and once you lose faith in yourself it's hard to recover.'

Lottie and Ed continued munching silently. Then Lottie turned to Archie and looking directly at him said, 'What happened, Archie?' Archie got up and threw a little pastry to a resting gull. He made no reply. Lottie and Archie exchanged knowing looks, but they pursued the subject no further.

'Anyway,' said Lottie, changing the subject, 'After lunch we shall take a peep at Mr De Quincey's cottage, see if we can spot any clues.'

Ed looked thoughtful, 'Do we have any other suspects?'

Lottie wiped her mouth with the back of her hand. 'Well, I've always wondered about those divers here for the summer.'

Ed interrupted Lottie: 'Oh, Robert and Mary Wakefield, they do go out at odd times and spent ages asking my dad lots of questions. Perhaps they're treasure hunters? There are lots of wrecks around the islands.'

Archie joined in, sitting down once more. 'My Great Aunt said that Captain Wilberforce may not be who he says he is: he has post delivered addressed to Harry White. Perhaps he's a spy or criminal? He doesn't have a boat, and he's a captain!'

Ed looked at Archie and grinned. "Who told Auntie Hettie that? Was it Mavis Penworth? She's such a gossip; that post could just be a case of misdelivery.'

Archie pondered their growing list of suspects, picking a worrying scab on his knee. He turned to Lottie. 'Why is it that you and Ed are so fearless?'

Ed picked out some moss from a nearby rock. 'Well, Archie, if we had fears, we wouldn't leave our cottage. It's about managing your limits. We swim, but not on a falling tide or in fog or rough weather. We climb, but not in high winds or blinding rain. We are cautious, not fearless. Lottie here, however, has some special skills, and I would never compete with her rock climbing; she is sure-footed but never careless.'

Lottie blushed at these compliments. 'I love climbing and my heroine is Gwen Moffatt; she's a champion woman climber, she's not in the kitchen making rotten pasties, she's got her boots on, scaling the heights in the Alpine peaks. That's going to be me, lads. Mind you, I might take a pasty with me!'

Archie and Ed laughed at Lottie, she stood aloft on her rock like a political speaker at a rally, waving her arms about. She jumped down and they all got up to make their way back to town and Headland Road where De Quincey's cottage was, super sleuths that they were!

Ed turned to Lottie as they made their way along Ocean View and suddenly stopped in his tracks. 'Lottie, what do you want with my clothes?'

Lottie winked as she replied, 'I'm going to become a boy scout next Wednesday and abseil down Rocky Point! Ed, you will be at the base. As it's low tide, you can reach it with your dad's punt, if you beach it. You wanted to report the news, well, this is your chance. Take the photo and put some news in the *Norwhel Times*, promoting you and me!'

Archie looked on, open-mouthed. 'You don't expect me to be part of this, do you, Lottie?'

Lottie laughed. 'No, Archie, you are going to distract my mother in the bakery'.Archie looked towards the heavens and groaned. 'To think I could have been halfway up a volcano in Guatemala!'

CHAPTER 19
A Close Shave and a Lost Parrot

The afternoon was getting cooler, the wind picking up as they came to a halt in Ocean View, beside the Island Hall and opposite Peter De Quincey's holiday cottage. There was no cricket today on the field behind the Island Hall; all was quiet, just two holiday-makers, blissfully unaware of the trio. The holiday-makers were preoccupied, bent over in the long grass opposite, searching for something. Ed made an assumption that they were hunting for the rare wild Pyramid Orchid. There was, however, more than a fine line between careful botany exploration and stamping on the poor flowers to extinction. At least their fervent hunting ensured the three sleuths went unobserved.

De Quincey's cottage was deserted. Archie, Ed and Lottie tiptoed around the back of the cottage, fighting their way through clumps of well-established Agapanthas that were tall enough to be a barrier: tall, thick stalks, luxuriant foliage and huge sky-blue flower-heads brushing against their shoulders. The garden was unkempt, very overgrown, and as a result guarded by a tall hedge of nettles, rather like Sleeping Beauty's castle. Braving the nettles, which they threaded carefully through, they found themselves at the back of the cottage beside a set of windows. They pressed their faces against the glass. Ed could make out what might be the kitchen/dining area of the cottage: a cooker, a small pine dresser, an enamelled sink, the bowl of which was piled high with dirty dishes. Beneath the window was a wooden table, its surface covered with various books and charts. The back door of the cottage was ajar and a stray thrush had flown in to perch on the water tap, staring out at the interlopers. Lottie was busy making observations as all three leant heavily against the stonework, hands cupped around their eyes like make-do binoculars, anxious to discover clues in the cottage's interior gloom.

Lottie, bothered by some ants and Nelson's wagging tail, was turning to explore another window when De Quincey appeared right in front of her. He shouted very loudly, his bulging eyes and red face meeting her blushing face. 'What do you brats think you're doing snooping around my cottage?' Ed and Archie visibly jumped and span round to face De Quincey. For a few seconds all three sleuths were struck silent, while Nelson yelped and ran for cover at the Island Hall.
'Well?' De Quincey continued. 'What a blasted nerve! I should call the law!'

All three stood poker-straight, red-faced, their backs now against the cottage wall, visibly shaken.

Archie started stuttering into DeQuincey's livid face, 'I've lost Captain Cook, sir.' Ed and Lottie looked at Archie open-mouthed at his quick-witted excuse.

'Who the hell is Captain Cook?' De Quincey exploded. 'What's he doing here? Are you thieves?'

Archie realised he had recently become quite adept at fib-telling, so continued in halting sentences: 'A parrot, sir, escaped, thieved....' Archie looked desperately at Lottie, like pass the parcel of excuses, and she responded with 'Underpants, sir!'

'What?' De Quincey was now super mad.

Lottie looked to Ed. It was now his turn to continue the chain of excuses. 'We've lost the parrot, and the care-taker of the Island Hall...' he pointed opposite at the building, 'told Archie he'd been spotted at your cottage.' 'Sir,' Lottie interjected hastily, 'We were concerned for your underpants!' Archie shut his eyes, hoping for the ground to swallow them up, and waited for De Quincey to explode further.

'What the hell have my underpants got to do with you, little girl?'

Ed winced as Lottie continued, 'Captain Cook is a prop-er thief, he steals anything, your underpants should be locked up.'

DeQuincey stamped his foot. The three shrank back in fear. This silver-grey beak-nosed ferret of a man was near breaking point. He raised his eyes to meet Lottie's and sarcastically hissed, 'Is this a case for the Foreign Legion, M.I.5 or Interpol?'

Lottie decided they were now in trouble and she should change the subject. 'Well, sir, he's always stealing, sneaking and swearing something awful, with words a child like me shouldn't hear!' De Quincey stepped back, obviously now enjoying this, and Lottie continued: 'Yes, sir, who knows where he goes? He visited me with Archibald's underpants, squawking *Yoobiraysya!*

Yoobiraysya! very suspiciously, and Archibald doesn't speak Spanish, do you, Archie?'

Before Archie could defend himself, De Quincey stepped forward, his face so close to Archie's that Archie could feel his breath and the smell of garlic.

'I'm not surprised, you idiot boy. *Ubiraysya* is Russian for 'get out'. Where did the bird get that from, Archibald?'
Archie went white and started shaking and stuttering, 'Captain Cook was a ship's parrot who sailed all over the world with lots of foreign sailors, who like me probably told the bird to 'get out'!' Archie was now breathing heavily.

DeQuincey stepped back and turned round towards his kitchen door. 'Get out, yourselves! You stupid kids, don't ever let me catch you here again, or, or....' He said no more, turned on his heels and went inside, slamming the door.

The trio literally fell over each other, crashing through the jungle of nettles, then crushing the Agapanthas, fleeing for the lives, along Ocean View with Nelson at their heels. They didn't stop until they reached Ed's cottage, gasping for breath, bent double, hands on knees, heads down. It was some time before they came up for air. They sat down on Ed's back door step, sweating and panting.

Ed was the first to speak: 'Did you see the charts on his kitchen table? What does he want those for, eh?'

Archie felt recovered enough to add, 'And the rope, charts and rope!'

Lottie looked at them both. 'I think he's highly suspicious and dangerous. We'll have to be careful. And furthermore, how come he knows Russian, eh? Artist, my aunt Polly!'

Archie looked thoughtful; it was probably time to return to Lighthouse Lookout Cottage and lie low for a while. As he stood up to go, he looked inquisitively at Lottie. 'Lottie, how did you know they were my underpants? A lucky guess?'
Lottie met his gaze and with a wicked grin said, 'Who else has a name tag in the waistband saying Archibald Fernando Bosworth!'

They all laughed uproariously, and the three sleuths dispersed for the rest of the afternoon.

CHAPTER 20
Friday, Knots, Boats and Crab Sandwiches

Friday morning was a 'blue day', the morning sun blinding Archie as he woke up. Hettie bustled in and Henry bustled out. Archie slipped on some shorts and a short-sleeved shirt and went down for breakfast. Hettie stood by Agatha preparing breakfast, but looked at Archie as he came in: his legs now covered with the full glory of nettle stings from De Quincey's garden.

'Where did you get those nettle stings, Archibald?' she quizzed him.

Archie went very red and added to his growing list of fibs by declaring, 'Nelson jumped up, tripped me up and I tumbled into them.' Hettie looked unconvinced and raised an eyebrow at Archie suspiciously.

Archie decided to change the subject with some speed: 'Oh, today's Mr Duffie's day off, he said I could visit him to find out more about the lighthouse.' Hettie once more looked at Archie with the other eyebrow raised, but he ploughed on. 'I'd like to know more about that...and...and...' Archie scratched his nose, but couldn't help thinking his Great Aunt was indeed psychic, for nothing escaped her.

Hettie went into the pantry and returned with a dozen eggs from Moor's Farm: 'For Mr Duffie; he may need eggs to make cakes... perhaps,' she smiled.

Archie grinned knowingly: eggs for cakes, no doubt! He went up to his bedroom to fetch the carved piece of driftwood for Mr Duffie's scrutiny.

Hettie looked at Archie's first attempt. 'Not bad, Archibald, not bad. Oh, by the way, Mr Duffie's down on Pasty Cove first thing; he's replacing some rowlocks. Do you remember your way?' Archie nodded. She continued, 'Drop off those eggs and your carving on the way, or my eggs will never survive the journey.'

Archie walked the path to Rocky Headland, dropped off his goods and continued through town before he had to turn along Sandy Lane to Pasty Cove. He passed Pawley's Bakery, and Lottie was just coming out with a bread delivery for The Lugger.

She grinned, 'How're your legs, Archie?'

Archie laughed. 'I'm sure Great Aunt knew what we'd been up to; she was very inquisitive.'

'Archie, you are so transparent, you always look guilty.'

'We all carry a bit of guilt, Lottie. After all, Scarlett Pawley, does your mother know what you need those boy's clothes for?'

Lottie punched him on the arm. 'Shh, Archie! The whole island will hear you!' With a turn of the heel she was gone, leaving an aroma of fresh bread behind her. As she turned away, Archie noted that below her shorts she too was displaying a red rash on her legs!

William was near the water's edge at Pasty Cove. The tide was rising, and he was bent over his punt at the water's edge, holding a screwdriver. As Archie approached, William looked up. 'Ah, Archibald lad, just in time: hold the punt steady while I secure the rowlocks.' The oars were lying inside the punt along with an aged set of rowlocks, one clearly broken, and he was in the process of fixing a new replacement.

'Right Archibald, I'll just tighten this a wee bit more; could you tie us up to that post over there, near that large granite rock?'

Archie anxious to help, tried to remember his scout knots. 'Is that a clove hitch, Mr Duffie?'

William grinned. 'Only if you never want to see the punt again, laddie. Come with me, bring the rope from inside the punt.' Archie picked up the coil of rope and walked with William to the post he'd pointed to. 'Archibald, the bowline is the king of sailing knots; perfect this and it could save a boat or a life one day.'

"Did your father teach you, Mr Duffie?' Archie asked.

'Nay, Archibald, my grandfather Thomas taught me. This knot has been in use for 500 years at least. If you get the hang of it, you will really impress the sailors on this island, and Scarlett Pawley.'

Archie blushed. 'Does she use it on the family boat?'

'It's a climber's knot too!' Archie couldn't believe how everybody knew everything on Teal! William formed a loop at one end of the rope, ran the end of the line back through the loop, then ran the line around the standing end and back through the small loop. 'Now, Archibald,

99

put the loop over the post. ' William asked Archie to pull on the rope, which he did and it held very firm. 'Now Archibald I'll loosen it and you give it a go.'

William walked back to the punt, picking up the broken rowlock. Archie tried to remember how Mr Duffie had tied the rope. By the time he returned Archie had tried his first attempt. 'It slipped, Mr Duffie.'

'You'll get it, Archibald. Now try again, back through the small loop, now pull.' Archie pulled on the rope, and it held firm. Success! His face lit up. 'Right, Archibald, George Trott is coming this way in his boat later and he's going to tow my punt to Smuggler Cove this afternoon.'

Archie looked thoughtfully at the punt. 'I've only been on a boating pond with a pedalo, that's my limit of seamanship, London is a long way from the coast.' Archie waited for several minutes, his stomach beginning to churn. It was not his intention to start boating skills this afternoon.

William put his hands in his pockets, and looked searchingly at the punt for some time. Then he took his hands out of his pockets, took off his blue woolly hat, turned to Archie and asked, 'Ever tried desert rowing, Archibald?'

Archie was completely at a loss. 'How can you row without water, Mr Duffie?'

William laughed, put his hat on Archie's head and told him to clamber into the punt. 'Right, Archibald lad, first rowing lesson: sit with your legs out straight, brace them against the middle seat there, now put the oars in each rowlock, that fixes them in firm, makes a pivot point to fix each oar in. Hold the oars at the handle end, now lift your hands a little to dip your oars in the sand. That will be water eventually, Archibald. Remember you will be rowing backwards, bow going forwards. Now, Archibald, pull back, push forwards, oars coming up, now drop your hands, brace, pull back. I hear you like art, Archibald. Imagine an ellipse, or oval shape, repeat that shape with the oars.'

Archie pushed forwards and pulled back as directed, then closed his eyes and repeated the movement in his head, elbows bent, knees bent then braced. He repeated this for a few minutes until William took his hat back and told Archie to clamber out. William put his hat back on, took the oars out of the rowlocks and returned the oars to lie inside the punt.

He stood up and put an arm around Archie's shoulder. 'Ach, come on, laddie, next week we'll do that in the shallows with a lifejacket on you. I'll be beside you in the water, holding the punt rope. We'll make a Teal boatman of you yet, Archibald Bosworth! Time for crab sandwiches and a large mug of tea!'

CHAPTER 21

Lighthouses on Dry Land and Strange Lights

William pushed open his cottage door and with a cackle went in. 'Enter the house of mirth, laddie, take a seat.'

Archie handed over the eggs that Hettie had given him, which he had left by William's gate earlier.

William went into the pantry beyond the front room, the smell of freshly baked cakes still lingering, making Archie's mouth water. He looked around him while William was busy getting lunch. The cottage was very much the same as his Great Aunt's: small windows, whitewash over granite block walls, low ceilings all fitted criss-cross with immense wooden beams. Beneath his feet was a flagstone floor, worn smooth through time. The furniture, however, was quite remarkable: strange assemblies of wooden parts made into new furniture. The chair he was sitting on was highly carved; Archie fingered the dark polished arms decorated with leaves and exotic fruit. The back was the same, but the seat he felt sure was a cupboard door! There was a selection of small occasional tables with carved tops but plain legs. A dresser behind him, near the cottage door, was constructed using the bottom of a punt, rather like a boat standing upright

and fitted with shelves. Archie couldn't help being reminded of men carrying coracles on their backs in sepia
pictures in encyclopaedias, rather like turtle shells. The
shelves of the dresser were littered with pieces of mis-
matched china, jawbones of long deceased fish, once
fierce but now benign, brass shell cases from the war,
ancient thick glass bottles, pottery sandwich paste jars
and even a few china dolls' heads. As Archie leant forward, he identified the dining table having once been a
huge wooden door: the only clue being a round hole and
keyhole where the doorknob and key once fitted.

William came in and sat down opposite Archie with the
sandwiches; Archie helped himself to one of humungous
proportions, so thick he could hardly fit it in his mouth.
But between mouthfuls he couldn't contain his curiosity,
and shook his head in bafflement: 'Mr Duffie, I have
never seen a home furnished like this! Not wishing to be
rude, sir, but looking around your home...'
William nodded: 'I know it must look like an explosion
in a furniture shop, where all the parts have landed in the
wrong place. All this furniture was beachcombed over
my 50 years as a lighthouse keeper.'

'I didn't wish to be rude, because it's fantastic. How did
you get it all?'

'Wrecks mainly: sailing ships had proper furniture in
state rooms and captain's cabins. Sometimes you find
bits on the beach, sometimes it's floating on the sea
around the lighthouses. The skill is making good use of
the things you find. For the last 70 years, when I've gone
beachcombing, scavenging, call it what you will, I would
find these bits and pieces,' he said, pointing to the furniture around them. 'I'd find a chair back, a door even,
pieces made of wood, even a holed punt, and decide
what it could be. This room, Archibald, is rather like a

furniture hospital! Ach well, lad, it's like this,' and William picked up the last of the crab flesh with a weathered hand, popping the crab into a mouth just open enough to consume it, between his splendid grey moustache and beard.

William recognised an interested audience, and leant back in his chair to relate a little knowledge about his life as a lighthouse keeper. 'I started as a Wickie when I was 16, for the Scottish lighthouses. In those days the light was gas, controlled by a clockwork timer that turned the light. But I had to be on watch in the light room by night, to make sure the light worked proper. Nowadays everything has changed; I'm just waiting to hear when the Teal lighthouse will be powered by electric, and that, Archie, could well be the last of lighthouse keeping as we know it.'

Archie sensed a sadness in the room and asked a question. 'Did you have to turn the light out during the war years?'

William perked up immediately. 'Ach, they were difficult times. We created a red light using the same lenses, and we painted grey bands on the lighthouse instead of red.'

'Were you ever bombed, Mr Duffie?' Archie continued.

'No, but the mines that floated in the sea to sink our convoys often floated by our lighthouse off Edinburgh. We were issued with rifles to shoot them if they came too close. They were frightening times, Archibald, and if there was enemy action we were isolated: no contact, even food got short.'

'Your wife must have found that really scary, Mr Duffie.'

'Aye, she did, Archibald, but we were all in the same boat, so to speak. We were grateful for quite small things: letters from home, fish from a passing trawler when the weather was bad and we couldn't catch fish ourselves. The sea gave us many gifts, including a crate of Russian vodka once! We rescued an airman one day who had parachuted from his plane after it had been hit; the rest of his crew perished. He had to live with us for a week until he was picked up by our supply boat. He was from Sarnia in Canada and his grandmother had taught him how to cook, so he repaid us by making cakes, especially these.'

With that William went into the kitchen and came back with a bag of Eccles cakes. 'I know your Great Aunt loves these. Tell her the eggs are grand and much appreciated; the Eccles cakes are a fair exchange.'
Archie reached into his pocket and with a little apprehension handed William his piece of carved driftwood. William turned it over, studying it. Stroking its smooth outlines with weathered hands, William looked at Archie: 'A fine fish, Archibald. What made you choose a fish?'

'It felt like there was a fish within it, and as I carved it, it sort of took shape.'

'You're a natural, Archibald. Did you copy it from a picture?'

'I didn't copy anything, but I remembered a drawing of a fish someone gave me a long time ago; it was a red and yellow smiley fish.'

'Yes, it feels like a happy fish!'

'Do you have children, Mr Duffie?' Archie asked.

'We had a son, Douglas, whose ship was torpedoed and sunk in the North Atlantic in 1941. He was a leading signalman.' There was a terrible silence after he said that. William took the plates and cups into the kitchen.

Archie didn't know what to say but the gap was soon filled by William, who said in a matter of fact way, 'Archibald, lots of folk lost someone; many lost a friend or family member. My wife Winnie took it badly and got sick. I lost her in 1946.'

Archie chose to broach a difficult subject; not looking at William directly, he asked, 'Do you ever get used to that loss, sir? You seem so content.'
'Ah well, laddie, we all deal with loss differently. I find keeping up communication with 'em is a good thing.'

'I don't understand, Mr Duffie.'

'Well, Archibald, I discuss boating and lighthouse duties with Douglas all the time, as if he's still around; and Winnie, she gets my household questions. That way I'm never alone or downhearted, and Winnie is terribly critical of my cooking, Archibald.'

Archie felt he could ask Mr Duffie anything; he didn't feel awkward or stupid, and Mr Duffie didn't treat him as an idiot. It was an odd feeling, but he felt safe with him. William chatted on about his life as a lighthouse keeper, the companions, the modernisation of lighthouses, war-time dramas.

Time passed quickly, and the sun was low in the sky when Archie said, 'I've kept you, Mr Duffie. I didn't realise what the time was.'

'Archibald, it's been a pleasure, and I'll be offended if you don't come back next week. Remember your second rowing lesson!' Archie laughed, 'I'll try not to sink the boat, Mr Duffie!'

William went into the back of the cottage and came back with some lengths of rope and another piece of drift-wood. 'Let's see what you can fashion with those, lad.'

Archie carried the Eccles cakes in one hand and his new projects 'to be' in the other. Before he left, he set his carved fish on the table and said, 'I'd like you to have this, Mr Duffie; call it a modest exchange for lessons learnt.'

William picked up the fish and placed it on a shelf on the dresser. 'I'll treasure it, lad.'

Archie coloured and hastily made to leave. He was just opening the door when William remembered something he'd meant to ask: 'Oh Archibald, can you ask your Great Aunt if she knows who would be using the Old Rope Shed? I noticed lights on in there last night. Maybe the scout troop on the island are using it. I had a quick look this morning, and there was a coil of rope and some empty tins of beans, so it's probably the scouts. That's odd, though: they usually let me know as I'm nearby, and they're due to visit the lighthouse on Monday.'

Archie said he would mention it to his Great Aunt, closed Mr Duffie's door and strode away down the path to Lighthouse View Cottage, a little lighter than when he'd started the day. As he walked, breathing the sea air, he remembered a crayon fish picture, given long ago. He sniffed and shook his head, but smiled at the memory. Feeling quite settled, Archie wondered if his Great Aunt would miss one of those Eccles cakes if he snuck one out now. Archie reflected what a perfect day it had been as he munched away on the path home.

CHAPTER 22

Rope Sheds and Abseiling

Hettie was dozing in her chair when Archie returned to the cottage, Henry asleep on her lap till he jumped up and ran to his food bowl. Archie put the Eccles cakes on the kitchen table and put the kettle on for tea. Hettie rubbed her eyes, stood up and brushed down her pinafore. Dinner was a shepherd's pie, keeping warm in Agatha the Aga. Without ceremony, Hettie took the dish out of the oven, put the dish on the table and handed Archie a second plate and fork. They both sat there as dusk fell, comfortable in each other's company.

Archie finished his first and took his dish out to the sink. Before he placed his bowl in the hot water, a scooped a little leftover pie onto Henry's dish, as he was so fond of Hettie's shepherd's pie. As Hettie finished off her supper, she called out to Archie in the kitchen, 'I hope you're not giving Henry any of George Trott's best mince, Archie!'

Archie and Henry exchanged conspiratorial looks as Henry cleaned off Archie's dish and Archie put it in the sink. 'It's all right, Great Aunt, my dish was finished.' A slight fib, but it was an accurate statement.

As Archie washed the dishes, Hettie joined him at the sink. 'Great Aunt, Mr Duffie wanted to know who was using the Rope Shed. He saw lights from there last night, and he assumed it was the scouts who are here on island.'

Having dried the dishes, Hettie started putting them away on the dresser in the front room and turned to Archie. 'I wouldn't think so, the scouts weren't due here until this afternoon. I saw they were pitching tents on the

Moor's Field his afternoon. I met the troop in town getting supplies at Porthmoor Stores: twelve lads and three adults, and when I went in, it looked like chaos, the stores were being besieged; the scouts were everywhere, opening jars, moving boxes, smelling the cheeses, and they were noisy little varmints too! One of them, a tall lanky lad with a face full of spots, told Rose that he'd not chosen his sweets yet and to serve the very old lady first.'

Archie waited patiently to hear about the Rope Shed, but asked her who the very old lady was. Hettie very nearly exploded, going very red in the face: 'He meant me, Archibald! What a nerve, now come on, am I a very old lady, Archibald?'

'Great Aunt, you will never be old to me,' Archie replied diplomatically.

Hettie laughed loudly. 'You sweet talker, you. I would have let you have an extra Eccles cake for pudding, but you've already had one!'

Archie grinned. 'How did you know?'

'Archibald, give a 12-year-old growing boy a bag of cakes, and they'll never bring the whole bag home!'

Archie settled in an armchair. 'So who would use the Rope Shed, and where is it?'

Hettie settled in the other armchair. 'It's along the headland from William Duffie's cottage, but it hasn't been used since after the war. Perhaps someone's sleeping rough there, but who?' Archie decided that he would tell the others tomorrow, but he could just have a peep himself in the morning to see if he could see any clues. He

110

needed more information. 'What is a rope shed? Is it a place to store ship's ropes?' Archie asked.

'No, they used to make ropes there, especially during the war; they've made rope there since I was a girl. The women spun the manila and the men put the yarn through special metal dies, that look a bit like circular sieves with big holes in. After they put strands together they then twisted them into rope.'

'Surely these islands didn't need so much rope?'

'Oh yes, Archie, rope making was an industry in the past, and even in the last war: hammocks for the sailors in the convoys. Even in olden times ships came into the islands wanting rope to repair their rigging. Since the arrival of the motor boat and peace time, there's not the need for much rope; they even use a plastic type now. But they'll be using proper rope tomorrow at Rocky Point for those scouts abseiling.'

'What's that?'

'Well, Archibald, if you don't want to jump off a cliff, you tie up to a fixed point and use the rope to sort of walk down the cliff backwards. They do it every year, part of their scout survivor badges.'

'How do you know so much, Great Aunt?'

'I used to run the Guides on a Wednesday on Norwhel, when I was younger, but our guides weren't allowed to do anything like that. Even now it's considered unlady-like: the guide movement keep to housekeeping, wood-land skills and first aid.'

Archie suddenly thought about Lottie and her wardrobe request: oh crikey, what was the mad girl going to do next!

The next morning Hettie left Archie porridge in the Aga
and walked up to Moors Farm to collect butter, milk and
clotted cream. Archie got dressed, sat down in Hettie's
chair to eat his porridge, spooning sugar on most of the
top layer, but leaving Henry's portion sugarless. As he
passed the bowl under the table with a cat portion left,
Archie licked his lips and the spoon, looking out of the
window and deciding if he should investigate the Rope
Shed on his way into town to meet Lottie. What harm
could it do, just a peep through the windows? And it was
on his way.

The wind was coming from the south-west, and whilst it
was a warm wind, the clouds were racing overhead like a
cine film speeded up. Archie left the gorse path from his
Great Aunt's cottage and took the path to Rocky Headland. But before he reached William Duffie's cottage, he
took a right turn through a clumped heather area where
the path was not so clearly defined. There were brambles
and nettles growing uncontrolled, in danger of taking
over the path; Archie wished he'd put some socks on.
The brambles showed signs of red berries, not ripe yet,
as some were still in flower.

After a few minutes, Archie came upon a long, low granite-built shed with a zinc roof, now completely shrouded in ivy. Unlike the island's traditional granite cottages, there were many windows on all sides of the building. Neglected for some time, nature had begun to engulf the building, so that like the roof, ivy covered many of the windows. Archie approached the Rope Shed from the headland side, while the other end looked out to sea.

Archie wondered about snakes in the long grass, or worse. He leant against one window, avoiding the nettles and brambles, cupped his hands, pressed his nose to the glass and peered in. He could see the old machinery this end, just as his Great Aunt had described it: filling this end of the building were a cross between a giant mangle and a series of giant discs with circular holes in. He could almost imagine what this must have been like, filled with local men and women splicing and twisting the yarn into ropes for the huge sailing ships that would fill the harbour in days of old. The window interior and the machines inside were festooned with cobwebs.

Happy to indulge himself in local history, Archie ventured to the next window, but suddenly trod on a length of dry wood that disintegrated with a loud crunch. All at once a face appeared at the window, from the inside: a ghastly nightmare face, pale white with a shock of blonde hair and eyebrows. Then their eyes met, Archie fell backwards into the brambles, his stomach turning over, feeling sick, and his legs shaking. The intruder's eyes were like a ghost train feature, both bloodshot, yet one eye was fixed and the other looked right. And then the face was gone and Archie heard a clatter of furniture before a door opened and closed with a resounding bang.

When Archie got to his feet, which was a few minutes later, he looked for the figure; but he or she was gone.

Archie couldn't summon the bravery to search inside; he ran back to his Great Aunt's cottage as fast as he could and fled into his bedroom. He lay on the bed, panting, his heart beating far too fast. At last he grew calm. He reached for his drawing pad and pencils and sketched the grotesque face he had seen. Was it the ghost of a rope maker from the past? He reasoned this, but concluded that ghosts passed through doors; they didn't knock furniture over or crash doors, they floated in white sheets. Would anyone believe him?

Archie looked at his watch: it was time to meet Lottie. He carefully folded the sketch and put it into his shorts pocket. There was safety in numbers: they would go as a team, Lottie, Ed, him and Nelson of course.
Stolen fuel, stolen punts and now a grotesque monster hiding in a disused rope shed! Something was afoot.

CHAPTER 24
Abseiling and Sleuthing

Lottie was waiting by the bakery door when Archie arrived. She was grinning as ever, hopping from one foot to the other in anticipation of their little adventure; but when she saw Archie's pale face, she stopped grinning.

'Whatever's the matter, Archie? You look like you've seen a ghost!' When Archie removed the sketch from his pocket and handed it to Lottie, she unfolded it and gasped, 'What's this, Archie?'

He leant against the bakery kitchen door frame and sighed deeply. 'Mr Duffie told me he'd seen lights in the old Rope Shed, so I thought I'd investigate a little. I thought it would be nothing.' Archie felt better now and his heart was beating normally. 'He was in there, Lottie. He looks dangerous. I'll never forget those eyes; I think one was a false eye, it stayed put looking at me, the other looked to his right and the door.'

Lottie took Archie by the shoulders. 'Whatever possessed you to go there on your own? Fine advert for 'fear of most things', Archibald Fernando Bosworth! You might have seen the person who is causing all the trouble on Teal. Is he in partnership with De Quincey? We'll have to tell the special constable on the island, Archie. However, I have somewhere I have to be. Go into my mum and tell her I need to run an errand for Judith Wyatt, the Reverend's wife. Mum doesn't like her: she says that my mum got the blame for the communion wine shortage. Ridiculous, my mum doesn't like any sort of wine, she says it's a posh person's tipple. So mum won't check up on me, Archie.'

116

'That's all very well, Lottie, but will she ask me to do anything?'

'Archie, you're a lad who confronts dangerous criminals. I'm sure you can cope with a few bakery challenges!' And with that, Lottie turned to go, a bundle of clothing in her hands. 'Ed should have the punt ready by now, let's hope he doesn't drop his Kodak in the sea!' Archie closed his eyes. Kodak? He often felt that since his feet had touched the quay steps on his arrival, his life had not been his own: either Lottie or Henry were orchestrating his life. With another sigh, Archie returned the sketch to his shorts pocket and went into Pawley's Bakery where Mrs Pawley was behind the counter, stacking loaves of bread on the shelf behind her.

As she turned round, she wiped her hands on her pinafore and looked at Archie, smiling expectantly. Archie explained that Lottie was running an errand for Judith Wyatt. It was at this point in his speech that Mrs Pawley stopped smiling, shook her head and snorted loudly. She folded her arms and started uttering phrases not usually heard in the Reverend's church, such as, 'dipsomaniac', 'pulpit prima donna'! Lottie was right, Mrs Pawley did not like Judith Wyatt at all!

Mrs Pawley took off her apron and put it on Archie, tying it up behind his back. 'Scarlett was supposed to be here. I've got to go to Suzanne Eggbert's for another batch of honey. I need to go now to get first dibs before anyone else. You can do Scarlett's job and man the shop while I'm away. Prices are on the shelves by the breads and cakes. Bags are by the till. Check your change before you hand it over, wash your hands and don't eat the profits!'

Archie washed his hands and stood, somewhat upright, behind the counter and waited for his first customer. In walked his Great Aunt, who laughed uproariously at Archie's poker face and and baker's apron, as if he was awaiting inspection in the cadets. Archie, red- faced, smoothed down his hair with the flat of his hand, straightened his apron and smiled politely. 'Yes madam?'

This was too much mirth for Hettie. 'Well, Archibald, trying out the retail trade, are we? I'll have a small cottage loaf and two Bakewell slices. Don't put the slices on top of each other in the bag, or the icing will come off on one another. Where's Scarlett, Archibald?'

Archie was finding it increasingly difficult to lie to his Great Aunt and looked out of the front window as he said vaguely, 'An errand for Judith Wyatt, she said.'

'Oh really, Judith organising a tanker of sweet sherry from Jerez, is she?'

Archie got the feeling that bad reputations were infectious in small communities, true or otherwise. However, he thought he had smelt alcohol on Judith Wyatt's breath when he went to evensong; probably her way of coping with all that shocking nasal hair her husband had, he thought.

Archie was pretty sure that Lottie had joined the scouts at Rocky Point for their abseiling session, as she had threatened. He was also pretty sure that she was in disguise. Why would she need Ed's clothes? What was Ed going to do with his camera?

As Archie leant over the treacle tarts, breathing in their syrupy aroma, Lottie was leaning backwards over Rocky Point. One scout leader was at the top of Rocky Point, another on a line midway down the cliff face and the third leader was on the beach at the bottom of the cliff face. Lottie had arrived ahead of the scout troop, Ed's woolly hat pulled down, just above her eyebrows and covering her ears.

Last night the scout leaders had enjoyed a social evening in the Lugger's Arms after they had pitched camp, leaving the boys settled in their tents with a scout youth leader until they returned after a game of darts. Molly, a somewhat chatty and curvaceous landlady, had taken a shine to the youngest scout leader, Nathan, and they stayed longer than they had anticipated.

It was quite dark when the three began to make their way back towards the Moors campsite. Contra to the scouts' motto of 'Be Prepared', these three were ironically not prepared. They couldn't remember the right path to the campsite, despite having earned their map reading and navigation badges, and decided to take a short cut through some fields. Nathan, still doe-eyed from Molly's attentions, was not paying attention; he fell in a ditch, and from the depths of a furrow declared himself to be quite incapacitated. The shadow theatre that ensued was worthy of an end of the pier show, as Phil and Frank supported him across the fields, stumbling themselves in the process. A less jovial trio arrived back at their leader's tent, where Frank applied a crepe bandage to his ankle, which was certainly more successful than Phil's triangular bandage! Nathan, they discovered, once inside the tent, had trodden in a farm animal's manure, which only added to the evening's drama.

As a result, our three leaders were not in a good mood this morning, and Lottie Pawley could have been a wallaby. They would not have noticed who was about to learn to abseil as they went through the instructions.

The rope which Frank, the patrol leader, had bought from the Chandler's was 120 foot long, and he looped it around a large standing stone as an anchor. With the two ends, he made Lottie stand between the two lengths. She then crossed the rope behind her back so they were in front of her. She then put them back together between her legs, holding the two ropes together on her right side. Frank asked his 'scout' which was 'his' strongest side. Lottie said nothing and put the ropes to her right; then, holding her breath, she leant back as far as she could, using her feet to push off and threading the ropes through her right hand.

Lottie was not nervous at all. She felt such a rush of adrenalin, which was sadly absent from her days in Pawley's Bakery! She was not nervous, for she believed that this was the first step towards her destiny. Her destiny lay in the Alps, the Himalayas, no more Cornish pasties or doughnut making, her 'rises' in the future would be provided not by flour mixes but by snowy peaks with meadows far below her.

Phil abseiled beside her, anchored to another rock; but with every foot he descended, and whilst concentrating on the task in hand in his capacity as Senior Patrol Leader, for the second time in 24 hours he was 'not prepared' for Lottie Pawley's unveiling.

The scouts had organised George Trott to pick up the lads in his boat to take them back to Pasty Cove, followed by a march back to Moor's Field campsite. Ed meanwhile was using his dad's punt and was on the beach as Lottie, on her final phase of descent to the beach, pulled her hat off, or rather Ed's, throwing it onto the beach. This scout had long red hair, blowing in the wind, her face flushed and grinning from ear to ear. Ed got his camera in focus and took a photo of her pushing off from the cliff face, red hair streaming behind her, grinning. The composition also, unfortunately, or fortunately, depending on which way you considered it, included Nathan's shocked, open-mouthed face, holding the rope at the bottom of the cliff face, looking up in horror as he realised this was not one of his scouts, but a girl!

Whilst Lottie was beaming with triumph at her subterfuge, and novice journalist Ed was preparing to send his photo and accompanying report to *Norwhel News*, there was no doubt that Lottie would be in big trouble when she got home; scandal travels swiftly in a small community. But at this moment Lottie didn't care, and Ed knew he had a cracker of a photo; it might even make a mention in *The Cornishman*.

At that same moment, Archie was enjoying the fruits of his labours in the retail trade. Mrs Pawley had weakened and let him have a slice of treacle tart!

CHAPTER 25

Limelight and Repercussions (Grounded)

Archie was just cramming the last of the treacle tart into his mouth, licking his fingers and wiping his mouth on his sleeve, when the door burst open. Lottie was nursing a sore hand from the rope, but it was as if someone had lit a lamp inside her. Ed couldn't wait to tell Archie about their escapade; he had been composing a journalistic account in his head ever since they returned his dad's punt to the harbour. Archie folded his arms and leant on the counter, shaking his head and looking at them both, his eyebrows raised in a non-plus way.

Lottie twirled around, her ponytail whipping round with her. She stopped mid-twirl and turned to Archie: 'What? What, Archibald Bosworth, with a syrup chin? Say something, congratulate me!'

Archie looked at her and shook his head again. 'Lottie, you are in so much trouble; the scoutmasters are in trouble; and you, Ed, did you ask your dad if you could use his punt for this stunt?'

Ed took a deep breath. 'Not exactly, Archie. I said that some of his pot lines looked odd and I was going to check them.'

It was at this precise moment that Lottie's mum exploded into the Bakery Shop. 'An interesting outfit, Scarlett. Go home now, and I'll speak to you later. You two, go now before I say something I'll regret! I don't know what possessed her! High jinks! Her place is here, we've a business to run. It's time she grew up and stopped looking for adventures. Why, I'd like the time to go and play the fool too! Why are you two still here?'

Archie and Ed left the shop with great speed. Mrs Pawley was still leant over the till shaking her head in disbelief when the door opened and Archie returned with Mrs Pawley's pinafore, mumbling, eyes downcast, 'Lovely treacle tart, Mrs Pawley, I really...'

Mrs Pawley looked up and stopped him mid-sentence. 'Archibald, go!'

Archie and Ed recovered on Pasty Cove, sitting in the dunes. Ed asked to look at Archie's sketch that Lottie had told him about. Archie retrieved it from his pocket and told Ed what had happened.

Ed was speechless and put his hand over his mouth in astonishment; then he stood up, looking down at Archie, still holding the sketch in his hand. 'Lottie's right, Archie. We have to tell the special constable here about this. The man is obviously up to no good, or he wouldn't be hiding in the Rope Shed and he wouldn't have run away. Pretty weird looking, isn't he? That whole glass eye thing, it's freaky, would have shaken me up, Archie. Fancy going there alone!'

Archie flushed. For once in his life he'd actually been brave. Surely his father would be proud of him now?

Ed and Archie left the beach and headed back to Archie's Great Aunt for advice; also for lunch, as Lottie was supposed to have planned sausage rolls as a celebratory lunch and both lads were hungry.

Hettie was picking beans when they opened the front gate. She wiped her hands on her pinafore and feigned surprise when she saw them. Gossip travels fast on Teal, and William Duffie had come to Lottie's back gate to tell her about Lottie's vaudeville act on Rocky Point. A fisherman had seen it all and passed William in his punt as he returned from the lighthouse this morning.

'Had a busy morning, boys?' she asked as they followed her through the pantry into the kitchen. Hettie produced the cottage loaf that she had purchased from her great nephew's retail apprenticeship, a tub of butter and a slab of cheese. As she started sawing through the loaf, she asked Archie to fetch a jar of home-made piccalilli from the pantry. As the boys sat down, there was a silent pause where all three looked at each other. Hettie got up and said, 'Right, lads, I'm fetching the lemonade; when I come back you can 'spill the beans'. Isn't that the modern phrase for telling me what's on your minds?'

Archie looked at Ed, who was at that moment devouring lunch as his first priority. 'Ed!' hissed Archie. 'You tell her!'

'Tell me what, Archie?' demanded Hettie, as she set down two glasses of lemonade on the table.

Archie reached into his shorts pocket, unfolded the sketch and handed it to Hettie. She looked at it, puzzled. 'Who is this, Archie?'

'He was hiding in the Rope Shed. Mr Duffie was right, there was someone in there the other night. I went up there this morning. I looked through the window and this man looked back at me. He looks dangerous to me, Great Aunt. Should we contact the special constable on the island? Remember all those fuel thefts and missing punts, it might all be connected. Also, when we looked through De Quincey's cottage window, he had charts on his table. Perhaps they are in partnership? What do you think?'

Hettie rubbed her chin, absent-mindedly cutting a slice of cheese and popping it into her mouth, followed by a spoonful of piccalilli. After a few moments chewing, she looked at the pair and said, 'I'll telephone Stuart Davenport and tell him to pop over this afternoon. You can make him aware of what you've seen. No more sleuthing! This all sounds very fishy and I don't want you getting into trouble. I mean danger, lads; this isn't comic book stuff. Keep out of it and let the law handle it from here on.'

Later that afternoon Stuart Davenport came round to see Ed and Archie. Stuart was very short with flabby arms, bald-headed but with a 10 strand comb-over across the crown of his head. He had huge sideburns, neatly razored beard and bandit-style moustache. Archie thought he was like a dressing-up doll where you stuck on all the facial hair. It was difficult not to want to stare at his hair adornments. He was on the tubby side, and one button had popped off his shirt revealing a fleshy, hairy midriff.

Stuart listened carefully to the account, munching his way through Hettie's rock cakes, wiping the crumbs from his beard and moustache, then stroking his sideburns. He deliberated on the sketch and the boys' accounts. 'Aunt Hettie, this isn't a lost bicycle or missing dog, this is a matter for Norwhel regular police. I'll go there first thing in the morning. Certainly looks suspicious. Can I keep the sketch? This chap's eyes are weird. Did you draw them right, Archibald?'

Archie was slightly irritated. He watched Stuart help himself to another rock cake and retaliated, 'I'm pretty sure it was a glass eye. After all, Ed, could you keep one eye still and move the other?'

Although Stuart Devonport wasn't watching as he munched, Ed did try to negotiate different directions with his eyes, to no effect, apart from Archie's amusement. Ed was disappointed with the special's response to what he considered dangerous felons on the island, up to no good. Ed continued along his line of investigation. 'Archie, I don't think I could fix one eye. Besides, that glass eye would make him very recognisable; also the blond hair. He could be foreign.'

Stuart Davenport drained the last of his second cup of tea and put his jacket on, which seemed somewhat tight. 'Don't you worry any more about this, lads. Sleep tight tonight; the strong arm of the law will sort this out!' With a last fond look at the remaining rock cakes, Stuart was reaching for the front door when Hettie reminded him that Deloris, his wife, was expecting her for a perm on Tuesday. 'Indeed, I'll remind her, Aunt Hettie.'

Ed knew that Stuart was relatively new to the island: he and Deloris had moved to Teal only ten years ago. Deloris had opened a hairdresser's on the High Street and Stuart was the Teal Island's telephone engineer. He also owned a smoker: Bob Woodley, who co-run the Porthmoor Stores, caught the mackerel for Stuart's smokers, and much of the product went to London. Everyone had more than one job on these islands. Deloris also did feet: if her husband ran a felons identity parade of folk's feet, she could identify them. **She knew feet!**

As Stuart Davenport left, Ed and Archie exchanged cynical glances. Ed broke the silence as Hettie saw Stuart off the premises: 'I don't know what you think, Archie. Let's talk to Lottie about this. What if whatever is taking place happens sooner rather than later? We need our own plan.'

Archie nodded and both took a rock cake as they considered a plan, strategically picking the sultanas off the tops first and flicking them into their mouths.

CHAPTER 26
Breaking Down!

Later that afternoon, Ed and Archie walked back along Moors Road to Lottie's cottage, Moors View. Lottie did not open the front door, but when they went around the back of the cottage, they heard a whistle. They looked up to see Lottie hanging out of an upstairs window, and the bundle of Ed's borrowed clothes descended on Archie's head. Ed could see that Lottie had been crying, and she explained that she was grounded for a few days.

Archie and Ed looked at each other. Ed spoke first: 'Lottie, we've seen the special constable. He says it's all in hand, but what do you think?'

Archie and Ed watched her disappear from the window. A few moments later she appeared at another window and without ceremony or notice clambered out backwards, finding a foothold on a nearby ledge across from the Pawley's pickling store, below the window. It was clear to Archie that this wasn't the first time Lottie had used this escape route. From the roof of the pickling store she stretched across to an old apple tree, no longer bearing fruit but sturdy for this exercise. Using practised handholds and footholds she was soon down at ground level, wiping her hands on the back of her shorts. Archie had ceased to be surprised at Lottie's antics and was somewhat in awe of her disobedience.

She looked at them both, 'Come on, mum won't be back for ages, she's catering for the R.N.L.I.'s women's group tonight, you know '*Jam and Jerusalem*'.'

Archie and Ed were at a loss with that comment: preserves and middle eastern cities? But like willing lambs, they followed her along Ocean View to the Island Hall. The sky was grey and there was a smell of rain in the air; the sea was flat calm, a sea mist forming. They looked around carefully, then went inside the hall. Like all properties on the island, the hall was unlocked. After all, how would the postman deliver parcels or the plumber mend your pipes? The Island Hall was once one of a number of WW2 Nissan huts, left behind by the RAF Air Sea Rescue Services, once the scene of dances, bowls nights and pantomimes. A number of other huts used as services barracks had been demolished, leaving just the foundations; but the building that now housed the Teal Island Hall had been constructed with pre-cast reinforced concrete, and even included an open fire, a kitchen with an oven and hot water. The islanders had laid a floor of shipwreck wood as a dance floor and even found the timber for a wooden stage, complete with requisitioned camouflaged net curtains for entertainment shows. Islanders had fond memories of the many romances initiated in the hall. Some men stationed here during WW2 returned and married local girls. George Trott was one such airman, stationed on Teal; George had met Macey at one of the dances when he was the camp caterer, then returned to marry her and transferred his skills to butchery when the war was over.

Lottie, still buoyant from her escapade, was keen to continue the trio's sleuthing. As they sat on the edge of the stage, their legs hanging over, Lottie swung her plimsolled feet backwards and forwards as if she was on a swing.

Ed, usually led by Lottie, was more hesitant: 'Don't you think we should wait and see what the Norwhel police do? They now have Archie's sketch; they could match it to mug shots of foreign wanted criminals.' Lottie considered the matter, handing round Spangles to Archie and

Ed, who sucked in silence. Lottie was impatient: 'The police move so slowly. How do we know there isn't a gang on the island?'

Ed, now in full journalistic flow, responded, 'Lottie, what would such a gang be doing on this tiny island? What input could we offer to stop them?'

Lottie, not to be interrupted, continued, 'This one-eyed man could be a master criminal, a murderer on the run, lying low until he can escape by boat to somewhere.'

Ed added animatedly, 'Well, Ireland or France are not that far away by boat. Just think about the fuel thefts and the missing punt, all lined up for an escape across the sea!'

Lottie was now in full flow: 'Oh yes, we could keep a watch out on the beach areas for imminent departures of suspicious strangers. We could tackle them. Look how brave Archie was!'

But Archie was silent, not swinging his legs in happy abandon. He had crushed his sweet almost immediately, and now bit his lip, looking at his dangling feet. With downcast eyes, he spluttered, 'We are not trained warriors, Lottie. Just because you abseiled down a cliff doesn't make you a match for a dangerous criminal.'

Lottie looked at Archie. 'I think I'm pretty tough. I'm an island girl; I know the landscape, the hiding places, I know the sea better than these interlopers, and Ed is a competent boat handler.' Archie gripped Lottie's arm and with a pinched face looked her in the eye. 'Lottie, I'm just a town kid. If it came to it, could I save you, Lottie? Could I, Lottie? I couldn't save my sister and I should have! I should have!'

Ed and Lottie looked on anxiously as Archie covered his eyes with his hands, his curly hair over his hands, his head bent on his chest, his shoulders slumped; quietly, he began to sob. Lottie watched Archie's shoulders shake as tears streamed down his face, dripping into his mouth, his nose running. Ed felt emotionally paralysed: he wasn't used to such outbursts of masculine emotion; personally, he wanted to march around the hall, describing its construction, how the military had built over a thousand Nissan huts for troops during WW2, also the unique back boiler of the fire, the thermal insulation in the construction...

Lottie, despite her iron constitution, crouched behind Archie, put her arms around him and cradled his head in her arms, rocking him gently until the sobbing subsided and he wiped his face and nose on his sleeves.

Ed had a terrible desire to laugh; he hated dramas, even though he read about them and wanted to write about them. It was different with strangers, they didn't matter, but Archie was a friend, and this was awful.

Lottie sat down beside Archie and put her arm around him. Gently she asked, 'What happened to your sister, Archie?' Archie covered his eyes again, without tears, almost afraid of remembering that afternoon. Two years of guilt and pain. Archie composed himself a little: he had never told a soul about it, just bottled it up. Ed now felt things were calmer and he could sound more empathetic. 'Tell us, Archie, we're your friends.'

Archie sighed deeply and, looking at the far wall as if he was recalling the scene, he began. 'It was two years ago: my mum, father, Susie and me went to Dartmouth Castle for the day. It was a beautiful day and we had fun, Susie and I running around the estuary area. Susie often got dizzy and mum told me not to over-excite her. We were playing hide and seek, and mum and father sat on a bank near the river setting up a picnic. It was Susie's turn to hide, but after a few minutes I couldn't find her. Initially it was fun and I called out, 'Come on, Susie, I'll eat all the jam tarts if you don't come out!' After five minutes I was getting angry. 'Come on, Susie, I'm missing my lunch!' I went down near the water's edge, where she was hidden by the bullrushes. I saw her blonde hair first, then her blue spotted dress with matching socks. Her eyes were closed as if asleep, one red ribbon fallen beside her, the other in her hair. Her sandals were just lapping the water's edge. I shook her. 'Come on, Susie, wake up, it's not funny any more!'

At that point, Archie hid his eyes and just sat still, tears running down his face, now a real mess. Lottie couldn't imagine what a terrible secret Archie had hidden from Ed and herself. 'What was it, Archie? Was it the dizziness?'

Archie wiped his eyes and sniffed loudly. Ed went and fetched a tea towel from the kitchen: he felt he should be useful, and he could put it back later. Lottie wiped Archie's eyes and face, now more composed, while he completed his account.

'The doctors said it was her heart, but Lottie, if I'd found her sooner, I could have saved her. But I didn't! I've tried so hard to imagine the scene differently in my head every day, if I'd saved her. My mum was heartbroken. My father carried her from the water's edge to the picnic blanket, silent, white-faced and rigid. I picked up the stray red ribbon and I've kept it ever since, afraid that I'll forget her. My father hides his grief and puts all his expectations on my shoulders. I have to be more. I'm sure he blames me.'

132

Lottie put her arm around Archie's shoulder again. 'Your father would have blamed himself, Archie. It was his job as her father to save her, not you; you were only ten years old.'

Ed now felt more able to help, since Archie was more composed. 'Archie, if she was sick, you couldn't have saved her. It could have happened any time if she had a weak heart.'

Archie looked up, feeling as if a world had been lifted off his shoulders. 'Ed, I feel I can never replace her. I can never be enough!'

Ed got down from the stage and stood in front of Archie. 'Archie, we three are misfits: Lottie can never be allowed to follow her dreams; I'm sure my father won't let me follow mine; and you could not save your sister. Your parents also carry that guilt, but you have to be free to be who you want to be, not what your father wants, or indeed what all our fathers and mothers want. This is 1958: perhaps we three can change our lives to become who we want to be.'

Lottie looked thoughtful. She got down from the stage, took hold of Archie's hand and pulled him down beside them. She put her palm down and motioned the others to put theirs on top, to form a star. Lottie gathered her rhetoric together, cleared her throat and said, 'Let's make a pact, Archie, Ed: no more guilt, no more fear. I vote we start with being look-outs and prove to our families that we are more than they think we can be. Agreed?' All three yelled together, 'Agreed!'

CHAPTER 27

Caves and Boats

The following morning Archie awoke to a dull, windless day; he snuggled down in his bed, watching the seagulls choreographing a fly-by for him. Henry was making some odd squeaking noises as they taunted him, his paws twitched and he licked his lips, contemplating a dessert course of parrot. It was a day for wasting time, creating fantastic creatures from the shapes of the clouds.

Lottie and Ed were lying low, both in meaningful employment: bread and crabs, no doubt. Ed may have looked penitent yesterday, but he was busy creating his introduction to journalism, 'Descent or Doughnuts'.[1]

Hettie brought Archie a cup of tea, placing it on the bed-side cupboard whilst simultaneously yelling, 'Get off the bed, Henry!' Henry promptly did so. However, as Hettie departed, he promptly returned to his former warm patch on the bed. Archie clambered out of his bed and located the rope pieces that Mr Duffie had given him for knot tying. He felt blissfully content back in bed: sipping tea, a purring cat, and practising knotting a few bowlines.

His peace was broken by Hettie bustling in again: 'Get off, Henry! Archie, Mr Duffie just popped by and wondered if you would like to visit again today.'

Archie was up in a trice, pulling back the bedclothes on top of the offending cat. He pulled on his clothes and clattered down the stairs for breakfast. He always started by reading the back of the cereal box; Henry liked corn-flakes too, so Archie leant down stealthily to place the remnants from his bowl under the table. He moved on to thick slices of toast, butter and Bovril. Hettie was in the kitchen listening to her favourite radio show, 'The Archers'. However, in the evenings when up in bed, he could hear his Great Aunt downstairs listening to Radio Luxembourg, a modern pop channel; she was not your normal 70 year old!

As Archie returned the cereal box to the table, Hettie returned to clear up and nudge Henry away from the Aga door. She asked Archie to pick some more sea beet for her, then added, 'I saw a clump on the headland above Smuggler Cove, so you won't need to venture onto the beach today.'

Archie replied through his last mouthful of toast, 'Of course.' He was relieved he didn't need to clamber down: that was an accident about to happen; he'd rather leave the rock climbing to Lottie. It also gave him more time with Mr Duffie.

Smuggler Cove was so near Lighthouse View Cottage that Archie decided to pick the sea beet on the way to Mr Duffie's. The day was still, the sea flat-calm, while Archie stood above the beach, looking down, remembering his first day on Teal and meeting Lottie. For a moment he just enjoyed the view of the beach, the ocean, the horizon, then bent down to pick the sea beet.

As Archie crouched down, he heard voices below. He couldn't see anyone, so carried on picking the beet. Then, through the vegetation, he saw a figure appear in the mouth of the cave near the right-hand end of the beach. He was tall, dressed in blue overalls and wearing wellingtons. The man looked briefly around him; when he turned around, Archie could make out his face. Not a young man: clean-shaven, a protruding chin and the biggest ears he had ever seen. In fact, Archie couldn't help thinking that he looked like a chimpanzee!

There was no doubt to Archie that he was acting suspiciously: the man turned back to the cave, went in and reappeared with a length of rope, a small anchor and a hurricane lamp. Archie remained crouched, silent and very still, watching the man go further along to the opposite end of the beach where he untied a rope from around a rock. Holding the end of the rope, the man waded into the water, pulled on the length of rope, hauling it towards him. Archie saw a small punt appear that had been around the corner of the cove, out of sight. The man placed the coil of rope, the anchor and lamp into the punt and carefully climbed in himself. Once seated in the punt, the mystery man picked up the oars and rowed away, out of Archie's sight.

Once the punt had gone, Archie stood up, beet in hand, and wondered what the man was doing so furtively. Who was he? What was he doing in the cave? Who was he talking to? A mystery indeed: one for further discussion with Lottie and Ed; and hadn't Lottie said to keep an eye on the beaches!

CHAPTER 28
Boats

William Duffie was at his gate as Archie arrived, and Archie dropped off the sea beet by the gate. He had brought a couple of bowline pieces with him, and he held them out to William as he greeted him.

William scrutinised them and said, 'We'll make a sailor out of you yet, Archibald.' He ducked into the cottage and reappeared carrying a canvas kitbag slung over his shoulder, and in the other hand a lifejacket. Archie did not have time to argue or ask questions as William licked his right-hand index finger, raised it skywards, looked up, squinted and declared, 'Ach, Archibald, it's a still, perfect day, no wind, flat sea, off we go, lad!'

He handed Archie the lifejacket and strode ahead. Just beyond William's cottage was a scrub area, where Archie followed closely behind William as the path became granite slab steps with a rope handrail to the left. Archie had no idea where they were going, but he could now feel the sea breeze from a beach close by. The steps descended and curved, winding down until they reached a small cove.

William reached down to grab a large metal ring attached to the bottom step, which had a rope tied to it.

William untied the rope and started pulling on the rope until a punt appeared through the shallow water, level with the step. William was suitably attired in black wellingtons, he stepped down into the sandy cove, wading ankle-deep into the water, bending down to hold the punt and its stern rope at the same time.

Archie was too speechless to say anything; he just had to trust William. His friend put on his woolly hat, which he had tucked in his pocket, and in a voice that showed his years of experience on the sea, he turned to Archie and said, 'Right, lad, put the jacket on, that's it: a strap between the legs, click it into the two waist straps you've clicked together, step into the middle of the punt and sit down, facing me. I've got the punt, Archibald; you're going nowhere.'

Archie stepped into the punt, it wobbled left, wobbled right and Archie feared he would be in the water soon.

'Sit down, Archibald,' William ordered. 'I've still got the punt.' Archie sat down, and although the punt was floating, it was steady.

William let the rope out a little, feeding the rope through his hands, still in control of the punt. 'Pick up the oars, Archibald. I've fixed them in the rowlocks. Now try a few strokes as I taught you on the beach.'

Archie dipped the oars into the water and made an ellipse shape, making sure that the movement of the left and right oars mirrored each other. To his amazement, the punt moved backwards in the water. William still held the rope but was now in front of Archie in the shallows. He held the stern of the punt, focused his gaze on Archie and asked him directly, 'Archibald, do you trust me?'

Archie was certainly nervous, but nodded. William stepped into the punt and sat down swiftly in the stern, bringing the knapsack and rope with him. 'Right, Archibald, you wanted to know more about the light-house, so that's where we're going: a five-minute row from here to the steps of the lighthouse. Off you go, I'll direct you. First lesson: port is left, starboard is right, dreckly is straight ahead; got it?' Archie looked up to the sky and repeated, 'Port is left, starboard right, dreckly straight ahead.' He started rowing, and for several minutes it was like watching an eight-year-old with a pedalo on Worthing Boating Lake – crazy circles and missed oars in the water! Archie laughed, the breeze ruffling his curly hair, and after a while he found he could respond to the directions. Although he was a strong lad, the physical effort made him puff and sweat; but for the first time in an age he felt strangely free, his cheeks glowing, his eyes bright and excited.

William remembered teaching his own boy to row, and was enjoying teaching this lad on the cusp of manhood; even a seal popped up its' head beside them to show its' approval!

CHAPTER 29
Teal Lighthouse

William was quite right: they reached the steps of the lighthouse after five minutes of hard rowing. Before William stood up, he asked Archie to pass him the rope which was in the bow of the punt. William then climbed out with the rope in hand, holding the punt steady, and instructed Archie to stand up in the middle of the punt. Still steadying the punt, William helped Archie out onto the step, then secured the punt by tying the rope to a metal ring anchored in the granite step. William retrieved the knapsack and led the way up the remaining granite steps to the lighthouse door entrance.

Archie removed his lifejacket, put it down in the punt, looked up at the lighthouse and caught his breath: the towering candy stripes soared above him into the blue beyond. Shielding his eyes, he studied the lantern at the very top. He was entranced: this was the stuff of boy's adventure books, this soaring building on a granite outcrop out in the Atlantic Ocean. He was marooned on a lighthouse island! There was a metal rail fence around the base of the lighthouse, leaving enough room for some wild flowers that survived in this wilderness: the result was a pretty frame of wild daisies, sea thrift and samphire, battling against the breezes.

Archie followed William through the entrance into what looked and smelt like an engine room. This was the power house of the lighthouse, where the diesel engine hummed away. He saw another type of pump, countless cases, boxes of stores and large tanks marked 'water'. Holding the metal handrail, Archie started to climb the spiral, concrete steps that led upwards. Whilst enclosed, Archie was not aware of the ascending height and he had the handrail for security. Circling around and upwards, the steps halted temporarily at a landing where a narrow doorway was open, leading into what looked like a bunk room. There were two beds, shelves with books, a small desk and a chair. As Archie looked in, what truly amazed him was that everything had been built to fit the round walls of the lighthouse! Archie noticed a photograph of a young man in uniform on the desk top: hazarding a guess, possibly Douglas, Mr Duffie's son.

He continued further up the spiral steps which halted again at another landing. A doorway led into the snug and the kitchen area. Accommodated into the round walls was a small kitchen range and a butler sink with wooden drainer. There was a small dresser against the wall and in the centre of the room, opposite the dresser, a small wooden table with two chairs. The white painted dresser had two open shelves, with china plates and dishes held behind a wooden rod, securing them in place. Archie imagined a stormy sea: shaking china would need to be secured. Cups hung from metal hooks under the shelves. There were two drawers below the dresser shelves, and two cupboards underneath. There was a place for everything and everything in its place.

William put his knapsack on the kitchen table saying, 'Lunch later, Archibald!'

Up they went again to the top of the lighthouse, to the lantern or light room. Archie looked around him, all 360 degrees. It was rather like being in a giant eyeball, giving onto the full view of the sky, with the sea far below. A bird flew by, so close that Archie could see its underbelly! The base of the lamp was turning, the thick lenses rotating, like some fairground ride without the wooden horses. The lenses were enormous, thick, multi-layered and curved. Archie felt detached from the land up here, up with the birds and the clouds. He couldn't help wondering whether a lighthouse keeper's life was lonely or not: it must take a particular character to manage the isolation. William stood by the rotating lens and addressed Archie in his official capacity as Teal Lighthouse Keeper: 'Archibald, when I first started as a 'wickie', we had to wind the clockwork motor every four hours'

Archie looked at William with growing respect. 'Why were you called a 'wickie', Mr Duffie?'

William looked out of the lantern window, as if addressing the sky. 'Well, lad, when oil lamps were used in the olden days, the young 'wickie' would trim the wicks, and the term stuck for every apprentice. Did you know that there have been forms of lighthouses since Roman times, Archibald? They used a simple fire in a basket placed on a tower. These days in the 1950s, our lighthouses are very sophisticated, diesel-driven. Every light has its own identification pattern and even the fog horn has its own unique sounds, so that ships always know where they are.'

Archie couldn't get enough information, and asked Mr Duffie how the foghorn worked: 'Well, lad, the foghorn

142

is somewhat different, operating on compressed air. Our foghorn is located in the engine room, but the horn blasts at low frequency notes: one long blast followed by two short ones.'

Archie continued asking, 'Mr Duffie, how far can it be heard? I've never heard a foghorn.' William was very animated. 'Well, it's weather-dependent, but always about 8 nautical miles away.'

Archie studied the huge rotating lenses beside him and asked, 'What about the lens at night? How far can it shine?' William folded his arms and, nodding at the lenses, continued, 'Not wishing to be too technical, these are called Fresnel lenses; they operate omnidirectional, all around.' Meeting Archie's eyes, he said, 'The light travels up to 16 nautical miles.'

Archie was silent for a while and then, looking per- plexed, asked, 'I've never heard or knew there was a difference between land and nautical miles. How does that work, Mr Duffie? Surely distance is the same. And what is a Fresnel lens?'

William loved to talk about his life of lighthouse keep- ing, and saw that Archie was a rapt listener. 'Fresnel lenses were discovered a long time ago. Basically it's a concentrated beam, focused by special multi-part spher- ical-shaped lenses. They increase the intensity of the light as it revolves on that pedestal. Pretty clever stuff, eh?' Archie agreed, pretty clever stuff, keeping shipping safe.

William put his hands in his pockets and returned to Archie's last question: 'A nautical mile, Archibald, uses distance that travels using the longitude of the earth, considering its curve. The light itself isn't aimed at the

143

land, it's aimed at the ship's level, about 40 feet up or about 15% more than a land mile.'

Archie marvelled at the lens, but William decided all this scientific talk had made him hungry. 'Come on, Archibald, time for lunch!'

They descended the spiral stairs, one floor down, and sat in the kitchen to share cheese and pickle sandwiches and a mug of tea. As William munched, he turned to Archie, picking a piece of pickle out of his moustache: 'Lovely pickle, made by the Pawley family; they have a pickling shed at home.' Archie raised both eyebrows and said looking down at the table, 'Lottie showed us the pickling shed yesterday...'

The two spent another hour or so looking around, literally, as each room was round! Descending another storey, they went down to the bunk room. Next to William's bunk, by the photo of Douglas, William said, 'We talk boats and stuff here, so I'm never lonely. I feel safe here, keeping other folk safe too. It's a grand job, but automation is coming. It will be retirement time soon. I'll miss my lighthouse life, Archibald.'

Archie looked thoughtful. 'What about writing a book, Mr Duffie? I'd buy it!' William grinned and put his head on one side. 'Aye, lad, that's an idea!'

Before leaving the lighthouse, William showed Archie the foghorn equipment. Archie bent down to study it, saying, 'I know I shouldn't wish for fog but it would be exciting to hear the foghorn.' William opened the door to the outside and replied, 'Not exciting for the ships, lad!'

Back at the punt, William untied the rope and held the boat steady. Archie put on the lifejacket once more, climbed into the punt, stood gingerly in the centre, sat down and put the oars in the rowlocks. William climbed in the stern and Archie made a better job returning to the Lighthouse Keeper's Cottage.

However, once back, William decided that Archie should have the whole experience. He beached the punt and told Archie to take off his sandals. Archie stood up slowly, stepped out of the punt and waded through the cold water, sand between his toes, helping to pull the punt up to the granite step and tie it to the metal ring on the step, with a bowline knot of course!

They went up the granite steps to William's cottage, where Archie returned the lifejacket and collected the sea beet he had left. As Archie was thanking William again, he mentioned the man he had seen at Smuggler Cove; he described him carefully, which made William thoughtful.

'Well, Archibald, the ears are a giveaway. I think that's Robert Wakefield. He and his wife are seasonal divers here. His wife is a Marine Biologist, studying coral reefs and seaweed.' William leant on his gate and laughed. 'Seaweed is good for fish, but bad news for boat propellers!'

Archie waved farewell and smiled as he was leaving, 'This was the best day of my life so far, thank you, Mr Duffie.'

William took off his woolly hat, ran his hand through his silver hair and declared with a smile, 'Ach, lad, a good day for me too,' as he went into his cottage and Archie made his way home.

CHAPTER 30
Sausage Rolls and Suspicions

Archie woke up to a loud purring in his ear. At first he wondered if his hearing had been affected by the sea yesterday, but when he opened his eyes there was Henry curled up in the bedding, his head on the pillow beside him! Archie heard Hettie coming up the cottage stairs just as Henry heard her too. He shot under the bed just as the door opened. Hettie, tea in her hand, was ready with her early morning command, 'Henry, get off the bed!'

However, Henry was not there. 'Oh, that's odd,' she re-marked, 'perhaps he's in the garden. Eggs and soldiers for you, Archibald when you get up. It's a blue day on Teal.'

Archie sat up, rubbing the sleep and the sun's beams in his eyes. A familiar rainbow was cast by the window onto the chest of drawers, the Ditty Box in the shade on top of it. He came down to a kitchen table laid with a jug of creamy milk, two boiled eggs in flowery egg cups, each on a flowery saucer with a slim spoon and knife laid beside them. To his left was a plate piled high with hot buttery toast, cut into fingers. Archie sliced the tops off the eggs with the knife and began slurping cold milk while dipping the toast into the golden yellow yolks. The last of the egg whites he scooped out with a spoon. Archie had saved a little yolk for Henry, which the cat licked off Archie's fingers, and while Hettie was in the pantry Henry licked the butter off Archie's plate, deftly done under the table.

Hettie came back to clear the table, stepping over Henry beside the Aga. 'Do you know, Archibald, I do believe that cat is putting on weight. What do you think?' It was

146

true that Henry was enjoying an enhanced standard of dining since Archie had arrived, but he set the limit at Henry getting into his bed! Archie decided it was time to leave, but he did at least offer to do some weeding later, so that Great Aunt could put her feet up in the garden. It was such a beautiful day on the island, and Archie strolled into town, cautiously popping his head over the bakery door. Lottie was behind the counter wearing a somewhat depressed look behind the very irritable Beryl Pawley; obviously Lottie's mother didn't share her daughter's climbing ambitions

Lottie's father, Jago Pawley, looked more malleable, and when Lottie's mother disappeared into the bakery kitchen, she put her head on her father's shoulder and whined, 'Oh please, dad, I'll just fade away if I don't get out in the sun today. I promise, no adventuring!'

It was amazing how manipulative a daughter can be to her father: he gave in immediately, saying, 'Off you go, young lady. Take some sausage rolls, but stay out of mischief!' Lottie tweaked her father's chin, with a cheeky reply 'As if!'

In a flash, she'd taken sausage rolls, put them into a bag and left the shop, linking her arm through Archie's. 'Come on, Mr Bosworth, let's call on Eduardo.'

Ed was at home painting the fence. He wiped his brow, obviously not enjoying the physical labour, and yelled upstairs to his mother, 'Mum, can I go to the beach with my friends? They need me!' Ed winked at his two pals.

Dot Trevethick's head appeared from an upstairs window. 'Edward Trevethick, you make sure you finish that fence tonight. It's a good job your father is sorting those pots out today, so he won't be back until later. Keep your eyes open, you lot, there's some queer goings on recently; a naughty water sprite perhaps?' she added sarcastically.

Lottie and Archie exchanged looks and Ed speedily put his paintbrush in to soak, took off his overalls, hung them up and came out of the gate with Nelson. Ed noted Lottie's bag and, nudging Archie, declared, 'Oh, how I've missed your sausage rolls!'

Lottie clasped them to her chest and said, 'First, gossip on Pasty Cove; then sausage rolls,' as Nelson scampered off in front of them, fighting imaginary sand monsters along the way.

Pasty Cove looked like a holiday postcard advertisement: blue, blue sky, turquoise sea, a little darker where clumps of seaweed lay below the surface attached to clusters of rocks; a beach of soft yellow sand, on which a fine line of tiny pastel shells and fragments of blue china left a decorative tidemark meandering along the beach. Nearer the water line, in the shallows, the sand lay in sculpted, rippled shapes, formed from the water's ebb and flow. The three wandered lazily through clumps of marran grass in the rolling sand dunes. As they reached the beach, they took off their sandals, then ran as fast as they could into the water, splashing each other wildly. Nelson meanwhile struck out through the shallows, to cool down. Thoroughly soaked, they all returned at a more leisurely pace to the dunes where Lottie had left their lunch.

They slumped down, their feet and ankles immediately coated in yellow sand, and they sat there, basking in the warm sun and their camaraderie. When Nelson returned, the sausage rolls were distributed, though Lottie told Nelson quite firmly that he couldn't have any. In retaliation, Nelson looked at the bag and their faces covered with pastry crumbs, then shook himself all over the three friends, the impromptu shower of water droplets spraying everywhere. Lottie squealed and Archie relented, giving Nelson a piece of his.

Once they were all de-crumbed and Nelson was lying in the shade, Archie told the others about his day with William. They were all impressed. Lottie declared, 'Well, Archie, looks like you're gaining more skills by the day. Rowing? Who would have thought it! Archie, you are, what's the word for changing from one thing to another, Eduardo?'

Ed looked up at the sky and said, 'I think the word you're looking for, Miss Scarlett, would be metamorphosis.'

Archie so laughed. 'I've become a sea monster.'

Lottie was very quick with her response: 'No, Archibald, just a monster!'

Archie giggled, then to change the subject, said, 'I saw something odd in Smuggler Cove yesterday. Mr Duffie said the person I saw was Robert Wakefield, a summer diving visitor.' Archie related what he had seen, and Ed confirmed the character analysis: 'If he had big sticky-out ears, that's Wakefield. He's odd-looking, reminds me of a chimpanzee.'

Lottie sat thinking, then added, 'His wife Mary was odd this morning: she came into the bakery and bought 6 pasties, 2 loaves of bread and 6 sausage rolls. That's why I didn't have enough for Nelson. Perhaps they're having a diving party.' Ed sat thinking. 'What's in that cave? You know, Archie, that cave was used by smugglers in the last century. If you go in at very low tide, you can still see the brass hoops from the brandy barrels stored there.'

Archie was intrigued. 'Smugglers, aren't they just stories? Surely people of Teal would have reported them, as it was illegal.'

Ed looked at Archie for some time before saying, 'Folk on Teal all got a share; that was their price for silence. And it wasn't just brandy either: silks, tobacco, lots of stuff.' Ed continued, 'It wasn't just smuggling, but ships were wrecked off these islands in the past, and the islanders survived on wrecked goods, anything that was useful. Our men rescued what crew survived, but we all shared in the booty. Beachcombing has always been a valuable pastime; after a wreck you could always pick up bits of broken furniture, china, timber; even, I'm afraid, drowned people, to whom we gave a decent burial. My grandfather once found a solid silver teapot and another time...'

Archie sat, mouth agape. 'That explains Mr Duffie's furniture then!'

Ed was deep in thought once more. 'My dad was out at Smuggler Cove this morning. Someone had cut his pot buoys adrift, cutting clear through the rope. He's furious. It's been a bad summer for rotten tricks. He's going back tomorrow to put that right.'

Lottie had been quiet for some time. She stood up, brushed the sand from her feet and in a business-like manner said,. 'Come on, you two, let's go to Smuggler Cove to see what we can discover.' With that, they all stood up and took the back lane along the High Street that faced onto the harbour, as Ed decided it was a good idea to avoid anyone they knew seeing them. From the quay, they walked across the lane that led to Headland Road and followed the path until they were treading through the heather, standing above Smuggler Cove looking down.

Lottie was the first to see something and shouted, 'Look at that! Someone has tied a rope to that tree and made an easy rope route down to the beach, to avoid the difficult climb up or down.' Archie and Ed looked down, but the beach was empty.

Lottie was unstoppable, and using the rope she went backwards down the steep rocky path to the beach. Lottie was a natural climber and she made the climb down look easy. Ed and Archie stayed at the top, avoiding the climb down, both somewhat nervous of who or what might be on the beach. All that talk of smugglers made them cautious.

They watched Lottie enter the cave, but she re-appeared after a few minutes and with no apparent trouble climbed swiftly back up to the top of the cliff to Archie and Ed. While Lottie caught her breath, Archie demanded, 'Well, what did you find?'

Lottie bent down to stop her stitch. 'Nothing but lots of footprints, and wheel prints from some sort of trolley. What would someone be using the cave for?'

Archie looked at Lottie and said quite slowly, 'Lottie this is not a matter for us. We're just kids. We should tell the special constable tomorrow. I promised Great Aunt I'd help her this afternoon, so I'm going now. Let's meet up again tomorrow morning and see him together.' Lottie did not look convinced, but even Ed tried to convince her: 'Lottie, we're in enough trouble already. Let's meet again in the morning.'

They left the beach, with Lottie looking back at the rope and saying to herself, 'Well, someone's fixed that there for a speedy access.'

Ed tried to placate her. 'It could be just tourists setting up a night-time beach fire for fun.' Lottie agreed. 'Well, it could be something quite innocent; we'll check again tomorrow.'

They left Archie at his back gate, and he went in to do a little weeding and some heavy thinking. It was certainly queer. Archie recalled Peter De Quincey's rope request at Porthmoor Stores: could it be the same rope at Smuggler's Cove?

CHAPTER 31
Full Moon and Darkness

Archie slept fitfully: one minute he dreamt he was sailing on a curving river, passing a hut on the bank and a one-eyed man fishing with an anchor. Archie tossed and turned, hearing Henry fall off his bed at least twice. He lay on his back watching the lighthouse light revolve and flash. Falling asleep once more, he dreamt he was watching his mother polish wellington boots, and then the boots were in Smuggler Cove, the water lapping over the toes as a chimpanzee pulled a punt to shore.

At last Archie drifted into a deep sleep, feeling Henry on his feet, also dreaming. There were colours drifting by like rainbow clouds; the clouds cleared and Archie was approaching the lighthouse door in a punt, but he was alone in the dark night. The lighthouse door opened and there in the light of a lamp was his sister, Susie. Archie sat bolt upright in bed. Susie looked so real that his heart was beating fast and he was shaking. He closed his eyes once more and then opened them. Why was it so dark? Henry was sat on the windowsill, looking out and quietly miaowing. Archie pushed his bedclothes back and went to the window. Where was the light? He waited for what seemed an eternity but was probably only seconds. The lighthouse light did not flash. Archie was not one for being impetuous, but that vision of his sister and the extinguished lighthouse light gave him a sense of danger.

Archie pulled on his shorts, shirt and jumper, pushed his feet into his sandals, crept quietly downstairs, located Hettie's torch on the dresser and left the cottage, closing the door quietly behind him. He switched on the torch, an arc of light illuminating the pittosporum hedge ahead of him, as with chattering teeth he headed for Mr Duffie's cottage. Archie just couldn't imagine why the light was out. His first thought was that Mr Duffie was sick, even though he had seen the light earlier that evening. Had the light broken? So many thoughts ran through his head as he rushed onwards in the dark, stumbling in some places where his torch light hadn't illuminated a rock in the path or a clump of gorse. In the dark, everything felt strange, silent, paths seemed longer without familiar landmarks; he felt completely disoriented.

When he arrived breathless at William's cottage, all was dark. He opened the cottage front door calling out 'Mr Duffie! Mr Duffie, are you OK?' Using the light of the torch, Archie climbed the cottage stairs, two at a time, but William's bed was empty. Archie felt like a burglar rushing through the house with his torch lighting up the bizarre furniture and china in its beam.

Archie left the cottage, closing the door behind him. What should he do next? As he opened the gate, he decided the logical thing would be to check William's punt. He used the rope rail to go down William's granite steps leading down to the cove. The steps were wet and Archie's legs were soaked from the long grass. His feet slipped more than once on the steps, the torch picking up the edges, casting shadows, sharp and wavering. Reaching the bottom step, Archie discovered that the punt was missing. What should he do? Should he hesitate? Was this just a maintenance hiccup? Should he assume that all was in order?

Archie stood breathless at the bottom of the steps, looking towards the lighthouse, the moon falling on the lantern, an unlit lantern. Wasn't this dangerous for shipping? Was he over-reacting? He remembered his dream. If he had got to Susie earlier, would she have lived? He felt Susie was taking him to the lighthouse. Archie closed his eyes briefly, then grabbing the rope he had used to climb down, he ascended the steps, brushing the wet shrubbery at a faster pace than when he went down.

Archie ran along the Headland Path to Ocean View, his heart beating fast. Gasping for breath, he tripped once and grazed his knee, but ran on to Ed's cottage. He went around the back of the cottage, picked up a handful of small stones and threw them at Ed's bedroom window. After a second attempt, Ed appeared at the window. Archie didn't even say a word, his white face and wide eyes told Ed everything. In what seemed like hours but was just a matter of minutes, Ed reappeared at his back door.

Ed took Archie's arm. 'Archie, the lighthouse light is out!'

Archie gulped and trying to get his breath responded, 'Mr Duffie's punt isn't at his cove. I have a terrible feeling, Ed, that he's in real trouble. Don't ask me how I know! We need to act immediately; we're not waiting to contact Norwhel police!'

Ed pulled on his sweater, picked up a flashlight from the porch and grabbed Archie's arm. 'We'll use dad's punt from the harbour. I'll row, Archie, you direct me using the flashlight and we'll go and check this out now.'

'We can't wake Lottie', said Archie. 'The punt will only take two and this may be nothing. We can make sure Mr Duffie's all right, then row back, tie up the punt and be back in our beds.'

'Archie, calm down,' said Ed. 'You look like you've seen a ghost!'

CHAPTER 32
Midnight Row by Moonlight

When Ed and Archie reached the harbour, all was silent: boats and punts tied up for the night. The High Street had been deserted, no wind, like a ghost town. Archie went down the granite steps using his torch, a stark contrast to his arrival on Teal. Ed was on the quay, his dad's punt tied up to one of the mooring rings on the edge of the quay, the punt floating on the water below. Using the flashlight, Ed untied the rope and took the end to the quay steps and stepping down, pulled the punt to the steps. Archie stood tight against the wall of the quay steps; Ed passed him the rope and instructed him to hold the punt steady while Ed got ready to climb aboard. Archie knew that if he let go of the rope, the punt would be gone and he would be left on the steps.

Ed stepped into the centre of the punt, sat down and secured the oars in the rowlocks. Archie, holding the rope, carefully stepped into the stern and Ed gave him instructions.
'As I start to pull away, squat.' Archie knew about the balance of a punt, and as Ed pulled away from the steps, Archie promptly squatted, still holding the rope. Ed handed Archie the flashlight and told him to direct him

around Rocky Point. As Archie used the beam to shine above the water's surface, the beam picked up Ed's face.

Ed decided it was time for some levity, even though he was scared himself. 'Like smugglers, eh Archie? All we need is a barrel of rum! Oh Archie, just a small point, you said you had a fear of water, but can you swim?'

Archie's teeth were chattering. 'I'm not scared of the water, Ed, just scared of drowning! I lost my confidence in everything after my sister died. But trust me, Ed, I won't let you down.' Archie returned the beam to an arc of light ahead, behind Ed to Rocky Point, which was coming into view. The two boys were silent for a while, the only sound being the oars dipping in the water and a breeze that flushed their cheeks with each pull forward. Looking at the sea in the moonlight, Archie thought the surface was reminiscent of black oil, so flat, so calm; there was no concept of depth, no hint of where the rocks were. The moon was full and played on the wake left behind the punt as they rowed forwards.

Ed was a competent boatman, but he was concerned for his apprentice passenger. 'Archie, if anything happens to the punt, we keep a plastic baling drum in the bow and you can always hang onto the fenders on the outside of the punt.'

Archie kept the flashlight moving all around them as well as forward in the dark, and in an attempt to retain calm, responded with 'If your boating skills deteriorate, Ed, and we finish up in the water, I shall use the baling drum to beat you with!' There was nervous laughter while the arc of the flashlight picked up the rope shed on the headland above them. Archie looked up, remembering his recent visit there, but had no time to recount it.

Ed suddenly shouted, 'Blessed seaweed, it's wrapped around the oar!' They stopped while Ed unwound the seaweed and in the darkness threw it behind him with a splash. Ed rowed on cautiously, as he knew there were rocks around this headland. Seaweed always accompanied rocks, and as it was low tide he could easily hit a rock no longer submerged. Ed rowed slowly: there was good reason there was a lighthouse on this headland – lots of dangerous rocks! They continued in nervous anticipation. Archie couldn't help thinking that Mr Duffie must be in trouble; Ed thought similarly, but said out loud, 'I know we're both anxious for William Duffie, but remember: if the light isn't working, it could cause a terrible accident. These waters are notorious for wrecks, Archie!' They were both silent, Archie breathing hard as they slowly approached the lighthouse steps. The flashlight picked up William's punt, tied to the bottom step. Archie handed Ed the punt rope, and Ed stepped out of the punt while Archie shone the flashlight for him. Ed held the punt steady as Archie followed Ed onto the step. Ed tied up the punt into the same ring as William's punt was secured, leaving the two punts gently rocking together. Archie and Ed stood by the lighthouse door. They looked at each other anxiously, and Archie noticed that all was silent: there was no hum of the diesel motor in the engine room. But in they went.

Archie sensed that Ed was scared: 'It's all dark, Ed. This isn't good. Take my torch. I'll go up first.' Archie held the rail with his left hand and, using the flashlight in his right, began to climb the winding stairs. His heart was beating so fast that he kept holding his breath.

Ed was behind Archie, and in the darkness behind him said, 'I'm scared, Archie, are you?'

Archie took a deep breath and said, 'More than you know, Ed.' Archie reached the doorway into the bunk room. He shone the flashlight in, but the bed was made. William Duffie's knapsack lay on the bottom bunk and his wellingtons stood beside the bunk. They both continued up the spiral stairs more slowly, both breathing heavily, the light picking up the shadow of the stair rail and their silhouettes on the wall. All felt disorientated in the dark.

Ed spoke again, behind Archie: 'Why are there no lights, Archie? There are none inside or in the lantern.' Archie didn't reply. His heart was thumping as he approached the landing and the doorway into the kitchen area. His stomach turned as he shone the flashlight into the room.

His worst fears were confirmed as the beam of the flashlight illuminated a shrouded shape lying across the floor, the two chairs overturned near the table. A broken milk jug was caught in the light's beam, a stream of liquid turned to a white pool ribboning across the kitchen floor. As the boys' shadows were cast on the wall of the kitchen, Archie put his hand over his mouth and cried, 'Oh William, no!'

CHAPTER 33
Archie Takes the Helm, and Ed Gets Talking

Archie stepped forward into the dark kitchen. Ed stood behind him, looking over Archie's shoulder. He now saw that the body on the floor was William Duffie. Ed stood paralysed. Archie bent over William and shone the flashlight on William's face: it was white as death, his eyes closed.

Ed felt he was about to cry, but standing behind Archie, he stuttered, 'Heaven help us. Is he dead, Archie?'

Archie told Ed to hold the flashlight, then bent over William, kneeling down, putting his ear to William's chest. It was moving up and down and he could hear William's heart beating. 'He's alive, Ed, but I think he's in a bad way. Give me the flashlight again.' Archie shone the light around the prone figure and concentrated on William's head, looking for an injury. 'Ed, look, blood from his head has trickled down his forehead. Someone has hit him hard.'

Ed grabbed Archie's shoulder and with a trembling voice said, 'What shall we do? Who would do this, and why?'

As Archie went to stand up, William groaned and mumbled, 'Warn...warn...'

Archie stood up and closing his eyes momentarily in this darkened room, high above the ocean, the black sea below, he felt he had to take control of the situation. Ed's face was whiter than William's. Timing and action were critical. Someone needed the light out, William had got in the way, and William wasn't the only thing in danger tonight: shipping! Ed had his head in his hands and kept saying over and over, 'What shall we do, Archie? What shall we do?'

Archie handed Ed the flashlight as William groaned again. 'Look, Ed, there's something bad taking place tonight. I'm sure it's about Smuggler Cove: the cave, the rope. William's right, it's our job to warn.'

Ed felt a little calmer knowing that William Duffie was alive. He'd never seen a dead person. He took hold of Archie's arm and said, 'What will you do, Archie?'

Archie breathed in deeply, then made a plan. 'Right, Ed, there's no light. It's dangerous and we have to alert shipping. We also have to get help for William. Look, Ed, he's semi- conscious, breathing well but he's had a knock on the head. He mustn't be left alone. Ed, you need to stay with William. Keep talking to him, it's important, Ed. If I remember rightly, my scout's first aid training told us to keep the patient communicating. Talk to William. You're good at that, Ed!'

'But Archie, what will you do?' Ed asked with a concerned look.

'Ed, I'm going to take William's punt, it's only five minutes to the Lighthouse Keeper's Cove, I know the way now, it's a calm night at sea, perfect for a novice like me. I'm going to contact your dad, Ed, he'll know the best way to get help for William.

Ed pointed towards the kitchen window and the dark night outside. 'Archie, that's a good idea, but what about the shipping?' Archie picked up the torch. 'Ed, keep talking to William. Whoever hit him also knocked out the diesel engine that runs the light. The engine was off when we came into the lighthouse, so I'm going to activate the next best warning to shipping. I'm going to set off the foghorn, Ed. William showed me how it works and that its unique sound pattern will help ships locate themselves. That foghorn won't just alert your dad, Ed; it should alert all shipping in the vicinity. It will also alert Teal and Norwhel that there's trouble. If there are dark deeds being done, we need everyone's help!'

Ed shone the flashlight on Archie's face, as he was turning to go. But Archie, what do I talk to William about? Cooking, fishing? I'm not a typical crab fisherman's son!'

Archie bent down, squeezed Ed's shoulder and said, 'What about all those facts you studied from the family encyclopaedias which drive Lottie and me mad! William won't fall into unconsciousness if you keep that up. After all, you're a budding journalist, so practise!'

Ed was wide-eyed, but shone the light on William in the darkened room as he heard Archie clatter down the concrete lighthouse stairs, past the bunk room to the engine room far below. Ed took a deep breath and said, 'Where shall we begin, Mr Duffie? Mr Duffie, this is Edward Trevethick, I'm here with my light in the darkness...' Ed, took a deep breath and said out loud, 'Oh help, Archie, where are you?'

163

After some hesitation, Ed began again. 'Mr Duffie, the Atlantic is a big ocean, as you know. But I bet you didn't know that new knowledge has found that 3% of ice in Antarctic glaciers is penguin urine! Oh Archie, hurry and get help!' Ed muttered, with some anguish.

CHAPTER 34
Fog Horn in the Moonlight
and a Run to Harbour View Cottage

Archie reached the engine room and used his torch to shine a beam on the compressor. He'd read about shipwrecks, and it wasn't all brandy and tobacco: it was about ships sinking and people drowning. This wasn't a scene from a 'B' movie; this was a matter of great importance.

He remembered the sequence: initiate the back-up battery for the compressor, then wait to hear if the foghorn would now work. He held his breath: suddenly, one deep tone of the horn sounded, almost deafening him. He put his hands over his ears as the next two short blasts rang out across the dark blue sea and the clear moonlit night. Success! Time now to row and get help.

Upstairs in the kitchen, in the gloomy darkness except for the flashlight, William Duffie groaned again. Energised by the foghorn, Ed believed he would expect help soon. 'I expect you know this, Mr Duffie, but early fog signals used compressed air, but powered by a horse.' William groaned again.

Archie left by the lighthouse steps, untying the rope that held William Duffie's punt. Putting the torch between his teeth with some difficulty, Archie stepped into the centre of the punt, squatted down, put the rope in the bow, put the oars in the rowlocks and began to row backwards, towards William's cove. The moonlight was a welcome illumination on the lapping waves, picking up the shapes of the headland and the cove across from him. As he rowed he talked aloud to William, as if he was there with him, giving him confidence. The oars made a reassuring dip and splash like a heartbeat, and Archie wished his own arms were quicker. But he kept to the regime that William Duffie had taught him. Sometimes he timed the dipping of the oars with the foghorn: on a still night such as this, even the creatures of the deep would surely be awakened. The journey seemed to take an eternity instead of a few minutes.

But eventually, with a splash, he was at the lower step, exposed now at low tide. A crab scurried away under Archie's torchlight as he stepped out of the punt onto the step. He retrieved the rope from the bow, tied the punt up on the ring with a bowline, as William had taught him. With a fast beating heart, Archie mounted the steps as quickly as he could. He didn't see the top step in the darkness and stumbled onto one knee, wincing as he got back on his feet.

Using the light from his torch, and a benevolent moon, Archie ran the whole track to Ocean View, towards Ed's Harbour View cottage, in double quick time. He felt he had been granted super powers tonight: his shoulders forced forward towards the path ahead, his feet driven as never before. As he reached the group of terraced cottages where Ed and Lottie lived, Samuel Trevethick was already at the open doorway. 'What's going on, Archibald? Where's my Edward? Is he all right?

Archie was bent double on the cottage doorstep, gasping as he tried to catch his breath. He grabbed Mr Trevethick's elbow: 'Mr Duffie has been hurt. Someone stopped the diesel engine, so the light's out. Right now Ed is in the lighthouse kitchen, looking after Mr Duffie. But Mr Duffie needs medical assistance urgently: his head is bleeding, but he's semi- conscious.'

Ed's father went back inside and came out with a maroon, the warning signal for the lifeboat. While he hastily pulled on a jumper and his wellingtons, Dot Trevethick appeared in her dressing gown in the doorway. 'Samuel, what's wrong? Where's Edward? Where's my boy?'

Comforting his wife, Samuel put his arm around her. 'He's safe, but William Duffie has been beaten and the lighthouse light is out.'

'Heaven help us all!' she cried, clutching a handkerchief from her dressing gown pocket.

Archie looked skywards as Mr Trevethick set off the maroon. It flew high into the night sky, exploded with a colossal bang and lit the sky above with a blinding silver light. 'Right, Archibald, that's the Norwhel lifeboat alarm. I'll phone George Trott now, the senior man, and tell him to get help from the coastguard. Their boat is the quickest way of getting to the lighthouse and getting in there. Poor William!' Samuel Trevethick went inside to call George Trott.

When he came back out, he asked Archie, 'Did you activate the foghorn, Archibald?'

'Yes sir, Mr Duffie had shown me how it worked.'

'Well, Archibald, a grand job. Your father would be proud of the good quick thinking on your part; and William will thank you for it too. Shipping safety, Archibald, is the first rule of these islands: keeping souls safe on the ocean tonight.' With that, Samuel Trevethick headed towards the harbour to meet George Trott.

High in the kitchen of the lighthouse, Ed saw the maroon lighting up the sky. He wiped away a thankful tear and continued his communications with William Duffie. 'Did you know, Mr Duffie, that we cry 15-30 gallons of tears every year? Not all mine, of course. Actually, babies are tearless, isn't that amazing. Oh, Mr Duffie, the maroon's gone up! My wonderful dad, he's on the case, not long now, hold on!'

Archie left Ed's cottage by the back gate, hoping to find Lottie at Moors View Cottage next door. As Archie looked up to alert Lottie to tonight's drama, her bedroom window opened. But it wasn't Lottie who appeared: it was Beryl Pawley's concerned face looking out at Archie. 'Where's my Scarlett?' she demanded, rather more angrily than Ed's mother.

'I don't know.' Archie shouted back. He now had a terrible feeling that maybe Lottie was indeed in trouble, as her mother suspected. Beryl Pawley continued her ranting as her husband appeared at the back door, sweater on, pyjama trousers tucked into wellingtons.

Beryl continued to rant from her elevated position. 'Wait till that girl gets home! I'll give her what for!'

Archie and Jago Pawley's eyes met, and Lottie's father looked as if he was in no doubt that his wilful daughter was in trouble. Archie called over his shoulder, 'Don't worry, Mr Pawley, I think I know where Scarlett might be,' as he set off back down Ocean View towards Smuggler Cove, the most terrible feeling of dread making him sick to his stomach. 'Oh, Lottie!'

CHAPTER 35
Bad Business at Smuggler Cove

Archie was breathless as he reached Smuggler Cove, his heart beating hard. He crouched down in the scrub and grass above the cove. The fog horn was still blaring, but the beach was empty, completely dark. He strained his eyes, scanning the scene for anything unfamiliar. Perhaps all this was a mistake? But finding William Duffie lying in the darkened lighthouse confirmed that something was going on tonight. It could be that he had been mistaken about Lottie's whereabouts, for she did not seem to be here. He was about to break cover and move on to Rocky Point, when there was movement by the mouth of the cave. It was difficult to see what was happening in the dark. Archie could hear that the tide was rising, the moon picking up the crest of waves coming onto the beach in the shadows.

Then, just as Archie was moving to go, a figure came out of the cave carrying a heavy object. He couldn't see what it was, or who it was, but the figure was struggling as he carried the burden out to the beach. Slowly, bearing the weight, the figure headed for the water's edge. A full moon suddenly revealed the mystery character: it was Robert Wakefield, the man he had seen previously, the man with the big ears.

Archie crouched down again and watched Wakefield go to the shore's edge. He watched him wave a hurricane lamp to somewhere in the distance, out to sea. The man then deposited his load at the water's edge. Like some ghostly scene from long ago, Archie heard a punt being rowed to shore. A woman, who Archie assumed to be Robert's wife, Mary, coasted to the water's edge and, without beaching the punt, rested the oars in the rowlocks and waded ashore barefoot. She then assisted her husband in lifting the bundle into the punt. Robert Wakefield waited until it was afloat and then waded into the water and gave the punt a push to set it afloat. Mary Wakefield sat down again in the punt, took up the oars and started rowing her mystery cargo away from the shore. Archie noticed that she was a proficient boat-handler as she rowed back confidently, but back towards what, or who? Such a small punt was certainly not bound for the open sea, that was for sure. In the darkness she was carefully avoiding all the pot buoys. Archie wondered if she was making a rendezvous with a third party, in another, larger ocean-going boat? The hurricane lamp signalling by Robert Wakefield must have told Mary Wakefield that she could return to Smuggler Cove. How many mystery consignments had she ferried back to this other boat? Who was she meeting? What was in those heavy sacks? Why would they need to carry out this operation under cover of complete darkness? Perhaps the pair didn't want the lighthouse illuminating their clandestine journeys. This had to be illegal; perhaps it was smuggling?

Archie watched closely as Robert Wakefield returned from the shore to the cave and went back in. After what seemed a lifetime, but was actually about ten minutes, Mary Wakefield returned to the shore, got out of the punt and beached it. The tide was rising and she hesitated before leaving it clear of the rising tide. For a moment all was quiet except for the invasive sound of the foghorn.

Then suddenly a figure came out the cave carrying another sack. Archie realised that this wasn't Wakefield. The person carrying this load with ease was slimmer, taller. It was difficult to work out who it was. Archie had a terrible feeling that it might be Peter De Quincey, the silver-grey, goatee-bearded, vulture-like man whom he had first encountered in the Porthmoor Stores, and subsequently outside his cottage. He watched the figure with the mystery sack, load it with some difficulty into the punt. The unknown figure then picked up the hurricane lamp and signalled into the distance. Before clambering into the punt, the mystery figure scanned the beach area as if there had been an unexpected noise.

At the same moment Mary and Robert Wakefield emerged from the cave together. The figure by the punt turned their attention towards the other end of the beach where Robert Wakefield had tied his punt to the large rock the previous day. The moon appeared once more to illuminate that end of the beach and that same rock, which still had a rope tied around it. But there was something else. It was, or looked like, the bobbing of an animal's tail, and it attracted the attention of this person, the person that Archie was convinced was Peter DeQuincey. This person had clearly seen the movement too. With great speed and intent the person ran down to the rock and pulled out whatever was behind the rock.

To Archie's horror, it was Lottie who emerged! The person grabbed Lottie's ponytail, yanked it hard and then dragged her, screaming, along the beach to the punt. As Lottie and the figure tussled on the shore, she fought with flailing arms, trying to escape, but the assailant was too strong for Lottie. Then, as the moon came out from behind a cloud, the silvery light picked out the assailants face. Archie covered his mouth to stop himself crying out. The mystery figure, lit by the moon, had a spectral white face and two mad eyes: one eye fixed to the shore, the other on Lottie. And it wasn't De Quincey; it was the one-eyed man!

CHAPTER 36
Battle in Smuggler Cove

Archie stood up and with all his breath screamed out to the cove below, to the vicious evil human being who was hurting his friend: 'Lottie! Lottie!'

The one-eyed man looked up towards the disembodied voice from the headland. He momentarily lost concentration, and Lottie squirmed away out of his grasp, falling onto the beach. But almost immediately Archie saw him grab Lottie by the arm again and force her into the punt. Archie, paralysed, watched in horror in those short seconds as Mary Wakefield ran for the punt and clambered in next to the one-eyed man, she too restraining Lottie by holding the back of her neck.

Archie, in a panic, thinking only of his friend, yelled as hard as his lungs allowed, 'I'm coming, Lottie!'

The rope that the three had seen yesterday was still dangling down to the beach below, the quickest access to his friend in trouble. But Archie was not Lottie, he was no abseiler. He knew to turn round and descend backwards, but he had no idea how to get down. In a blind panic, and without plan or ability, he grabbed the rope with both hands and slithered and tumbled backwards, his legs striking granite rocks as he plummeted down to the beach.

Archie picked himself up from the beach, pain searing his left leg and his hands burnt from the chafing of the rope. He limped towards the shoreline, seeing the one-eyed man pick up Lottie and forcefully throw her back in the punt as she had wrestled free, now afraid for her life. Mary Wakefield shouted something at him; the one-eyed man screamed back at her, and Archie heard the familiar word '*Ubiraysya!*' In a flash, the one-eyed man screamed out and pushed Mary Wakefield out of the punt and into the sea, with an immense splash. Archie kept running towards them. Lottie had meanwhile used her opportunity, as Mary Wakefield was pushed into the sea, to try to escape. She tried to clamber out of the punt as it was pulled further out into deeper water. Archie could no longer feel his legs, or his chest pushing his body forward towards the punt and Lottie.

He watched in horror as the punt moved further away with Lottie in it, now struggling with the one-eyed man who was trying to row furiously while restraining Lottie, who was punching him. As Lottie made another frantic attempt to escape over the side of the punt, she almost unbalanced it, to stop this maniac abducting her with his weighty booty which was slowing them down against the tide. As the punt became unstable, the very worst thing happened before Archie's eyes. In slow motion Archie watched as the one-eyed man picked up an oar out of the rowlock and with some force brought the oar down on Lottie's head.

With a gentle roll, Lottie could be seen slipping silently over the side into the water, face down, floating on the black ocean, like a patch of bladderwrack, drifting out to sea. The one-eyed man began to row away with manic strokes towards his rendezvous, leaving Lottie drifting, motionless.

Archie passed Mary Wakefield as she stumbled, gasping, ashore. Archie plunged forward into the ice-cold Atlantic waves, his body hitting a submerged rock as he surged forward. He swam like he'd never swum before, using his arms like oars, pulling himself along, cursing that he couldn't make his body work faster. There was saltwater in his mouth and his ears, making him spit wildly. He was desperate not to lose sight of Lottie in the dark ocean, drifting away.

'Susie, make me go faster!' he screamed.

All at once, the moon appeared from behind a cloud and the moonlight picked out her floating body. He propelled himself towards her, reaching nearer with every stroke. Then all at once, with one last surge, he'd got her! He turned Lottie on her back, and himself on his back, with one arm under Lottie's chin, frantically keeping her head up. She felt so cold, so still. Archie headed back for the shore. On his back, in the blackness of the ocean, he felt so alone. He scissor-kicked his legs and tried using side stroke, forcing himself to find some strength to ferry his precious cold friend towards the shore. He seemed to be swimming for an eternity, panic rising within him.

At last he approached the shore of the cove. He heard voices, saw flashes of light. His tired legs grazed sand and he was at the shore. With the last of his strength, he picked up Lottie's, limp, cold body in his arms and gently placed her on the sand. He bent over her, his eyes swelling with tears as he put his head to Lottie's chest. He heard a heartbeat, but she wasn't breathing.

As if in a dream, Archie heard ship's hooters, saw arcs of light and was aware of screaming from the headland above. Archie remembered a picnic two years ago and his father's last desperate actions. Archie knelt over Lottie, tilted her chin up, pinched her nose and opening her mouth met her lips with his, as he pushed his own breath into his friend. Beryl Pawley was screaming 'Scarlett! Scarlett!' from the headland, and there were crowds somewhere, but Archie was alone in his world.

'Breathe, Lottie, breathe!'

Once more he opened Lottie's mouth and put his mouth to hers; tilting her head back, holding her nose, he exhaled all that was in his young body into hers. Within a few seconds, Lottie's chest went into spasm and she coughed up the ocean from her lungs, gasping for air.

CHAPTER 37
Archie's in Trouble

All his strength gone, Archie collapsed to one side of Lottie as she gasped for air, as if this was the first breath she had ever taken, her whole body trembling.

Archie felt confused, as if in a world of mist where mad lights searched, hooters hooted, whistles, fog horns and a tumult of human voices, all was dream-like. To his left he thought he saw Peter De Quincey leading a hand-cuffed Robert Wakefield towards a boat on the shore, his wife wailing behind him. This must be a dream or a nightmare.

Suddenly he felt a hand on his shoulder. It was Ed saying, 'Archie, Archie, are you all right? Help is on its way for Lottie: a stretcher is being roped down from the headland. Archie, you saved her! You saved her, but where is she bleeding from? Did she strike the rocks? There's a lot of blood, Archie!'

Archie felt that searing pain in his leg again, and he felt his world go dark. He slumped against Ed as Ed screamed, 'Oh help! It's Archie, he's bleeding badly. Someone help him!'

CHAPTER 38

Archie Remembers

When Archie came to, he remembered being carried, the
smell of salt air, moisture on his face and the sensation
of the rising and falling of the sea. He heard muffled
voices, 'Stay with us, Archie, just a few minutes.' The
rising and falling stopped, then distant voices as he was
lifted up steps, lifted, lifted...

'Well, good morning, Archibald,' said a familiar voice
beside him. Archie opened his eyes: he was in a hospital
somewhere. His leg really hurt, actually most of his body
hurt. Ed was helping himself to one of Hettie's rock
cakes on the bedside cabinet and opened a newspaper
noisily.

Archie tried to sit up, but with no effect. A very rotund,
rosy-cheeked nurse, Megan Lord, helped him up and
propped a pillow behind him. Archie was aware that his
left leg was heavily bandaged, and his elbow and his
wrist. 'Crikey, Ed, it's the wrong time of year for Hal-
lowe'en. What have I done to myself?'

Ed lowered the paper, raising his eyebrows up and down
in a ridiculous clown-like fashion, rustling the paper at
the same time. He cleared his throat and read out, 'This
trio of youngsters single-handedly stopped a maritime
theft of unbelievable treasure, lost for centuries. They
rescued the lighthouse keeper, Mr William Duffie; and
one lad, Archibald Bosworth, saved his young friend's
life after she had been left for dead by a notorious fanat-
ical treasure hunter...blah, blah, blah. This first-hand, on
the spot account is reported to you by cub reporter Edward Trevethick of Teal island. And look, Archie, I took
a photo of the Wakefields being hauled away by the po-

lice.' Archie winced and raised himself up on his elbows to get a better look at the report. He took in the newspaper photo and the three photos of Lottie, Ed and himself. Perhaps he was still dreaming, perhaps he'd died on the beach. He put the paper down and with a confused look said, 'I didn't see any police. I thought ridiculously that Peter De Quincey was involved with the Wakefields. Which paper is this, Ed?' he asked, still feeling dozy.

'*News of the World*, old man, we made the front page!'

Just then, the hospital ward door swung open and a man who shared certain similarities with Peter De Quincey came towards the bed. 'How are you feeling, young man? What a night, eh!'

Archie rubbed his eyes with his good arm. 'You can't be!'

'What can't I be, Archibald Bosworth?' grinned the slim man. Archie stared: it was the same De Quincey, but with short dark hair, clean-shaven, check shirt and beige trousers.

'Are you De Quincey?' asked an incredulous Archie.

The slim man sat on Archie's bed and patted Archie's good arm. 'Well, actually I'm Inspector David Herrien-Brown of Interpol. I've been undercover here for a few weeks. We'd been tipped off about this Russian chap, Georgio Dorikov. You kids almost blew my cover, but it was that ruddy parrot that confirmed our suspicions.'

Archie and Ed stared at each other, open-mouthed, and then turned to this Inspector. 'What about the parrot?' they both said with astonishment.

The Inspector leant across Archie, helped himself to one of Hettie's rock cakes and with a scattering of crumbs falling on Archie's snow-white sheets said, 'That parrot flew in one day and dropped a 17th century gold coin on my kitchen table. It was Spanish gold, part of a haul from Peru being transported to Mexico by one Captain Thomson. Captain Thomson intended to bury it on Cocos island in the Pacific, but en-route for Cocos, British pirates attacked his ship. They were repelled, but managed to get away with some of the jewels, solid gold crowns, chalices, even swords encrusted with jewels and of course gold coins. Though never confirmed, it was believed that many voyages later their ship was wrecked and sunk in the Atlantic, both crew and treasure going to the bottom of the ocean.

'The Wakefields found it quite innocently, while undertaking some marine biology off the coast of Teal. But last night, having brought their haul up in a few stages, they were transferring it to a ship further out last night, a Russian ship. My guess is that Dorikov is a thug working for a Russian oligarch and the Wakefields were expendable, as was Scarlett Pawley.'

Archie sat there, mouth agape. 'It was smuggling, like in a pirate book!' he declared, grinning widely. After a moment, questioning the Inspector, 'Can I just ask sir, what you wanted the rope for that you were trying to get in Porthmoor Stores? Was that rope for Smuggler Cove?'

Inspector Herrien-Brown rose from the bed, picked up another rock cake, winked and said as he turned to leave, 'For a washing line, Archibald!'

CHAPTER 39

Star Gazing and Hot Dogs

It was a clear night, the sky full of stars. Archie put his hands behind his head, lay back and sighed deeply. 'Did you ever see such a sky, you two? Magical!'

Ed, arms by his side where he lay, looked up and said, 'Of course those stars twinkling up there started twinkling billions of years ago. It's old light really, not fairy dust at all.'

Lottie, lying next to Archie, leant over him and hit Ed on the head with a cushion. 'Shut up, brainbox, your knowledge is driving us all insane!'

Archie looked up at the sky again and said, 'Well, Norwhel's hospital nurse, Megan Lord, told me that when they brought in William Duffie from the coastguard's boat, they thought he was delusional as well as concussed.' Archie left a space for theatrical effect. 'Seems he told Megan about penguin urine in icebergs!' Archie laughed and laughed.

Ed sat up and said, 'All right, mock me, but at least he didn't fall unconscious!'

Lottie turned on her side and grinned. 'Bet there were moments when he wished he could!'

The trio were sleeping under the stars in the back garden of Lighthouse View Cottage for their penultimate night together before Archie left to go back to London.

Lottie lay back and with a dreamy voice said, 'I don't care if it is old light or not, it's beautiful. Look, one of those stars is just glowing.'

Ed sat up, propped on his elbows. 'That's Sirius, the Dog Star, and if you're looking for the brightest star, it's the North Star.'
Archie strained his eyes to look. 'Where is that, Eduardo, font of all galactic knowledge?'

Ed, for once able to offer useful information, said, 'Archie, find the Plough: it's a line of stars that look like an old-fashioned plough, got it?' Archie located it. 'Right, follow the line from the Plough; there at the end is a really bright star, and that's it.'

Lottie looked up, sighing. 'It's so beautiful, everything is perfect. The other night I saw a shooting star and made a wish.' Both boys turned to her in the darkness, snug beneath their blankets. 'It came true. My mum was so relieved I was OK that I'm going on a junior climbing course in the Alps next May, and being sponsored by the Pinnacle Climbing Club of Great Britain, which is an all-female climbing club. And to make things even better, while I'm away, my brother is helping in the bakery and mum is starting him in the shop after Christmas!'

Archie turned to her in the candlelight. 'That's amazing, Lottie!'

Ed sat up and, unable to contain his excitement, declared, 'And that's not all, *The Cornishman* newspaper are accepting pieces by me on the islands and on island life generally as a cub reporter. I thought dad would be mad, but he said, "Yes, well, son, we'll see how long that lasts. You'll still want to be a crab fisherman, you'll see, lad!" Well, this Edward Trevethick won't give up; next term I'm going to start a school newsletter for the islands and learn a new unusual word every day!'

Archie congratulated Ed and started a chorus of 'For he's a jolly good fellow', followed by impromptu imitation trumpet noises. The trio then lay silently together until Archie spoke again. 'Actually, Ed, we shouldn't be too hasty about the benefits of crab fishing. If your dad hadn't repaired those pot buoy lines in Smuggler Cove earlier than he'd planned, Dorikov wouldn't have got caught up in the lines, so that the lifeboat could corner him and trap him. There was a customs man on board and I heard he had a gun! Not only was that amazing, but George Trott, refreshing his British Navy skills from the war, was taken to the lighthouse in the island pilot boat and using a fireman's lift, putting William Duffie across his shoulders, carried him down the lighthouse steps and put him into the boat which took him to the hospital on Norwhel. George Trott then boarded the customs boat at Norwhel, which went to arrest the captain of the Russian boat anchored some distance off Smuggler Cove; so that involved lifeboat, coastguard, customs boat and island pilot boat, amazing!'

Lottie got up and went over to the garden table to locate some more hot dogs. She returned with three more and squatted, handing out one each. They munched in silence, Ed moaning that his was too hot to eat. After two mouthfuls he commented, 'Did you know that hot dogs were a German product called *Daschhund Wursten* in the late 19th century? That's why the English for those funny short-legged, stretchy dogs with long ears is sausage dogs!'

Lottie lay down again and with a snort said, 'I bet I know something about hot dogs that you don't know!'

Ed was intrigued, 'Go on, Lottie, what?'

'Well, Ed,' she began, 'Henry's pinched the last two on the table!'

Archie yelled out, 'Henry, you greedy tom cat, leave our supper alone!'

Ed leaned towards Archie, wiping his mouth of grease from the hot dog. 'Where is our beloved Auntie Hettie?' Archie leant back, smiled and told them both, 'Auntie Hettie's been looking after William Duffie since his attack. She's cleaned his Aga, and they've made cakes together!' They all giggled.

Lottie turned to Archie, who had now closed his eyes. 'Archie, what you did to me, when you saved me, how did you know that? I've never seen it done before. My mother thought you were kissing me goodbye!'

Archie grinned. 'You should be so lucky, Scarlett Pawley!' There followed a brief silence, then with some seriousness Archie continued, 'When we found my sister, my father tried it on her. But her heart wasn't beating; yours was.'

Lottie was quiet for a moment. 'But Archie, where did your father see it done?'

Archie breathed deeply. 'Shortly before my sister's death, he was investigating an active volcano in Kamchatka, Russia. The U.S. Marines who were there with the *National Geographic* performed it on volcano victims whose lungs were full of volcanic gas. My mother told me the U.S Marines developed it after some war or other. I'd forgotten all about it on that day of the picnic, until I brought you to shore.'

Lottie looked at Archie in the dark. 'Does it have a name, Archie? Is it 'Mouth by Mouth' or something scientific?' Archie was silent until, turning on his back again, he answered, 'It's called "The Kiss of Life".'

All three were silent as Lottie reached for Archie's hand and said, 'Well, Archibald Bosworth, it saved mine!'

Archie turned to them both and, putting his and Lottie's hand on to Ed's, said, 'Nonsense, you two saved mine before that!' A somewhat emotional silence followed as the trio reflected on their summer adventures and friendship together; a summer that had changed all their lives.

The silence was rudely broken by a certain parrot which flew closely above them all, squawking 'Sacre Bleu'. He was swiftly pursued by a furious Henry, whose half sausage had been stolen by the parrot. Without invitation or hesitation, Henry jumped all over the trio as chaos ensued and the moment was gone.

CHAPTER 40
Leaving Teal

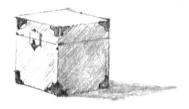

Archie spent his last night in his bed at Lighthouse View Cottage watching the light of the lighthouse revolve around, its flashes lulling him to sleep for the last time that summer. The next morning he packed his bag carefully, tucking his memory box in the bottom, with its many treasures: shells, knots, china pieces, carvings, a mermaid's purse, a National Courage Award medal and, twirled on top, a piece of scarlet ribbon.

Henry sat to attention by Agatha the Aga, Archie feeding him a goodbye breakfast treat, a piece of his leftover sausage. Henry entwined himself around Archie's legs, then with his usual post-food detachment, strolled out into the September sunshine for a well-earned rest on the garden bench.

Archie opened the gate of the cottage for the last time, patting it lovingly; it had been quite a summer. He was now to call his Great Aunt by her honorary Teal title, Aunt Hettie. William and Hettie walked along the scrub path with Archie, before turning onto the cobble stones leading to the quay.

Archie was very embarrassed: there was quite a crowd on the quay side, so he took his time along the cobble-stones. He still used a walking stick, as he'd needed 10 stitches in his leg and 4 for his arm. Beryl Pawley put her arms around him, giving him an enormous kiss. George Trott shook his hand, as did Samuel Trevethick. There was a lot of hugging, kissing and hair ruffling, goody bags of cakes and sausage rolls. Ed and Lottie smiled but stood back, somewhat embarrassed to show their affection in public for their friend. The *Demelza* captain, in his sou'wester hat and coat, presented Archie with a bucket for any seasickness. How they all laughed! As Archie was about to descend the granite steps to the lugger *Demelza*, Ed stepped forward and shook his hand vigorously. 'Archibald Fernando Bosworth, you're OK, if a bit dodgy at shrimping!'

To which Lottie added, next to him, 'Yeah, and rubbish at making pasties!'

Archie handed Lottie a large rolled-up sketch saying, 'For you two, a Saturday memory.' Lottie leant towards him as she took it, blushed and kissed him on the cheek. A whistle went up from the crowd.

Archie climbed aboard *Demelza*, the rope was untied from the capstan, fenders pulled in and the boat moved away from the quay. He waved a sad farewell and yelled, 'See you next year, Aunt Hettie!'

As the boat disappeared from view and all their arms ached from waving, Lottie unrolled the drawing Archie had given her. Ed peered over her shoulder. 'Oh look, Ed, it's doughnut Saturday on Pasty Cove, with all three of us and Nelson!'

In contrast to Archie's arrival on Teal, he returned stood at the bow of the lugger and breathed in the last of this landscape and seascape. He tried to photograph the lines of the rocks in his head as the lugger rose and fell, leaving a gentle wake behind the stern. The seagulls seemed to sing a different song for his way home: it was joyful. He watched with some humour as the captain, Jeremy Legg, puffed his pipe with his right hand while his left hand both steered the boat's wheel towards Norwhel and grasped a pasty at the same time. Reflecting on fond memories, Archie thought back to his morning of pasty-making with Lottie in Pawley's Bakery, and smiled.

As the boat neared Norwhel quay, Archie embraced the scene: the small boats, punts, fishing boats, the coast-guard boat, customs boat and of course, dominating the scene, buoyed up beyond the lifeboat slip, the RNLI boat in all its distinctive orange and blue livery: the boat and crew that had trapped a particularly nasty thug.

As the captain tied up the boat to the quay, Archie collected all his belongings, including a packed lunch for the

188

train from Beryl Pawley. Jeremy Legg shook his hand as Archie stepped off the boat onto the granite quay steps, saying, 'Come back again soon, lad. We're glad you've found your sea legs!'

Archie took one last look at the quay and climbed aboard the Norwhel transfer bus for the airport. No uncertainty this time: when the bus reached the airport, Archie clambered confidently into the plane. He ducked as he went through the clamshell-style door and found a seat by the window. Once settled, he peered through the window as the plane's engines roared into action. He sat back in his seat as it gained height, turning twice before rising above Norwhel. Archie craned his neck in every direction, looking for familiar landmarks. Norwhel and Teal were now a microcosm of hedged green fields, rocky headlands and golden beaches. They looked so small from up above, but so huge when he was actually on the islands. He craned forward again, to get a last view of the archipelago. He felt very emotional, and some words from a school lesson came to mind: 'This other Eden, demi-paradise ... this precious stone set in the silver sea.' This matched his feelings exactly.

Soon they were flying above the sea: a miniature fishing boat beneath them, rising and falling with the waves, and an oil tanker far on the horizon. Archie looked directly below, at the crested rolling waves, and found it hard to believe, as he unconsciously scratched his healing leg, that he'd really dived in that water. Had the people of Teal Island only known that Archie had declined this year's swimming lessons at school and had watched the life-saving sessions from a pool side bench! As the plane travelled onward, Archie looked back one last time at the little group of islands growing more distant by the second, and once again his heart ached.

Once on the train, Archie settled down in his window seat, facing forward, raising his poorly leg to rest on a newspaper on the opposite seat. The stitches were due out next week and were pulling and itching at the same time. He snoozed, wisely avoiding the turbot on the train's lunch menu, tucking into Pawley's sausage rolls instead, creating a flurry of pastry debris down his shirt.

The train stopped at a few stations, and Archie sleepily noted the holiday-makers returning to their cities, the Tamar bridge at Plymouth, then Brunel's coastal stretch beside the sea between Torquay and Dawlish Warren. This was where Archie had his last view of the sea, and the ancient iron wreck from WW1, enduring, peeping out of the water at low tide, rusting slowly in an estuary beside the railway line. On Archie's side of the train, on the other side of the estuary, was a small harbour, and the fishermen's 'watering hole', Ye Olde Anchor Inn. Then the sea was gone.

All too soon, the metropolis buildings, offices and rear gardens of terraced houses were flashing past the train window. Light was fading as the steam train hissed its way into the platforms of Paddington Station, London. Archie gathered his belongings together, the train and he having reached the end of their journey. He heard the train guard announcing, 'All change, this train terminates here, this is Paddington, London.'

As the train came to a halt, Archie reached out of the open window, pulled the compartment door handle down and opened the door. He picked up his case and knap-sack that William Duffie had given him as a parting gift, complete with four pieces of rope to continue practising tying knots and two pieces of sea-worn driftwood for carving. Using his walking stick, he carefully stepped down from the train, avoiding the gap, onto the platform.

The train was still hissing and filling the platform with steam, making it difficult to locate the barriers.

Meanwhile, an anxious mother and father waited impatiently for the familiar view of their son: a son who, on his departure at the beginning of the summer, was strained, pale and sad, his shoulders stooped, head down; as he had looked back at his mother, there had been such a heaviness hanging over him. They strained their eyes to pick him out of the disembarking passengers, amidst the banging of train doors, guards' whistles and clouds of steam enveloping them all. There were journalists and a photographer waiting for Archibald Fernando Bosworth, but Archie didn't notice them as he searched for the familiar frame of his mother.

Then the steam suddenly cleared and there, striding along, grinning widely, was a tanned, slightly dishevelled young man, unruly hair, sockless and limping a little, but shoulders back, eyes bright, somewhat taller than when he departed.

Archie's father stepped forward ahead of Archie's mother. He was rushing now, and embraced his young son as if he'd never hugged him before, so very tightly. Archie's mother was close on his heels, leaving the press behind as she put her arms around them both, tears streaming now.

They were three people lost in their own moment, oblivious to all, the station fading into insignificance. The press used that photograph on their front page, with the caption, 'Family United At Last!' And so they were!

Acknowledgements

My thanks to Jane Hamilton who generously gave me permission to use, John Hamilton's drawings, taken from his 'Sketching With A Pencil' book, inspired by the Isles of Scilly. Jane's father, John Hamilton was a renowned marine artist. He loved the Isles of Scilly and is remembered fondly by all who knew him.

Isles of Scilly artist, Ian Dunn, kindly gave me copyright to use the painting for the front and back cover. Ian's studio is the White Gallery, Porthmellon, St Mary's. This painting was one of a series, where Ian invokes the atmosphere of the Scilly Isles for inspiration.

My son Duncan was 'encouraged' to use his drawing talents to creative purpose. He produced the map of Teal Island and numerous freehand drawings to illustrate the storyline.

My granddaughter Katherine navigated and steered my husband Ron, through the stormy sea of technological difficulties.

Whilst my husband Ron did not want to be mentioned, it is without doubt that without his calm support, hard work and encouragement this book would still be in my desk drawer.

The *inspiration* for this book came about because my autistic granddaughter, Elizabeth is unable to read. The book was based on the Isles of Scilly where she lives, so that she could connect with the story, as I read it to her.

Whilst the book has been edited, should there be any errors I take full responsibility for them, 'to err is human...'